NIGHTSTALKERS!

Alone in a room with three t'Tant, the deadliest creatures on the planet! Dumbfounded, I stood stock-still for a long moment, not moving until the nearest t'Tant was within inches of my face, its claws outstretched.

I ducked down, under the desk, pulling my shoulder bag with me. One of the t'Tant landed behind the desk and began clawing at the bag, trying to get at me. As the t'Tant slashed the bag to ribbons, spilling the contents over the floor, one of its claws drew a long gouge down my left arm, ripping my tunic.

There was no way out. I couldn't hold the creatures off for long. My fingers scrabbled on the ground, looking for some weapon, something, anything that would buy me a few more seconds of life.

They fell on a concussior; I snatched it up. Maybe, just maybe, it would shock them, stun them just long enough for me to get out. I thumbed the concussior and flicked it out into the room, squeezing myself further back into the recess, fighting to keep the t'Tant's claws away from my face.

The concussior went off, deafeningly loud. Then everything went black. . . .

Ties of Blood and Silver

by

Joel Rosenberg

A SIGNET BOOK

NEW AMERICAN LIBRARY

NAL BOOKS ARE AVAILABLE AT QUANTITY DISCOUNTS WHEN
USED TO PROMOTE PRODUCTS OR SERVICES. FOR INFORMATION
PLEASE WRITE TO PREMIUM MARKETING DIVISION,
NEW AMERICAN LIBRARY, 1633 BROADWAY,
NEW YORK, NEW YORK 10019.

SIGNET TRADEMARK REG. U.S. PAT. OFF. AND FOREIGN COUNTRIES
REGISTERED TRADEMARK—MARCA REGISTRADA
HECHO EN CHICAGO, U.S.A.

SIGNET, SIGNET CLASSIC, MENTOR, PLUME, MERIDIAN and NAL BOOKS
are published by New American Library,
1633 Broadway, New York, New York 10019

First Printing, September, 1984

1 2 3 4 5 6 7 8 9

PRINTED IN THE UNITED STATES OF AMERICA

for Robert Lee Thurston

Acknowledgments

I'd like to thank the people who helped me both with and through this one.

During the writing and the rewriting, Harry F. Leonard and Mary Kittredge gave me much valuable criticism—as did my editor, Sheila Gilbert, who still knows how to make something better. Any flaws in the work are mine; many virtues are theirs.

I'm also grateful to Cherry Weiner, my agent for this work, as well as Kevin O'Donnell, Jr., Mark J. McGarry, Irene and Ken Herman—the best in-laws on the planet—and, most particularly, my wife, Felicia. Many thanks, folks; your advice and support are always appreciated.

Extract from *Delavesta's Revised Pocket Encyclopedia of e Thousand Worlds*, Earth-Normal Edition (New Ameri- n Library, 2519; LOTW Call #NSR2404098.1):

Quikref: **OROGA**		
Mass:	6.537e31 grams	(1.094 × Earth's)
Density:	5.968 g/cc	(1.081 × Earth's)
Radius:	6.395e8 cm	(1.004 × Earth's)
Surface gravity:	1064.415 cm/sec2	(1.085 × Earth's)
Escape velocity:	11.77 km/sec	
Year:	142.045 Earth days/	
	113. 55 local days	
Sidereal day:	29.942 hours	

Oroga is the sole habitable planet of Kaufman's Other Star (Freusen Durchmusterung Catalog #4322210351.093), a red Kl star with a luminosity of .252, mass of .725, and radius of .78 relative to Sol. . . .

Oroga's mean orbital radius is 7.176e12 centimeters— approximately .48 astronomical units. While the di- ameter of the primary is roughly three-quarters that of Sol, its apparent size is much greater from the surface of Oroga than Sol's is from Earth: Kaufman's Other Star occupies almost nine-tenths of a degree of the sky, appearing to be roughly three times the size that Sol does from the surface of Earth.

The planet's orbit is almost perfectly circular; the eccentricity is only 0.00059.... Combined with its low inclination of 5 degrees, this makes Oroga virtually seasonless.

The atmosphere is breathable without either prosthetic aids or surgical modification ... it is slightly richer in oxygen than Earth's (26%), poorer in nitrogen (72%), and richer in carbon dioxide (.035%); it contains large but not unhealthful quantities of argon, xenon, neon, and sulfur oxides....

The planet is 73% seas.... Of the three major land masses, only a small portion of the most northern has been settled by humans. The remainder are populated by t'Tant, the native quasi-sapient (see Appendix for qualification).... Since the t'Tant have no established civilization, population estimates of the native lifeform are based on orbital photo sampling.... Estimates range from less than one billion to more than 1.5 billion.

The majority of the human population lives either in or within one thousand kilometers of Oroga's single city, Elweré, although there are agricultural townships scattered throughout the inhabited continent. While the last official census gives the population as 259,276, it counted only citizens, those who actually reside in Elweré; residents of the areas immediately surrounding Elweré—Middle City and Lower City in the local parlance—are not legally citizens of Oroga ... nor are the workers of the valda and food plantations....

The actual human population of Oroga is believed to be approximately four million. There is a transitory schrift population, almost exclusively members of the metal-and-jewel-worker's schtann, who provide hand-crafted jewelry for the Elwereans. There are believed to be no other permanent sapient residents. . . .

Elweré is a robust and successful trader in the Thousand Worlds marketplace, importing large quantities of electronics gear, medicines, plastics, luxury foodstuffs . . . artwork, and building materials—the latter due to political considerations as opposed to lack of resources, in view of the great quantity of untapped ore deposits. . . . Simply, the Elwereans prefer to have as small a local manufacturing base as is possible, with most building done by work-contracted nonresidents. They can afford to indulge this preference. . . .

While there is some export of local silver . . . the Orogan economy is supported by the export of valda oil, the product of the beans of the valda plant (*Xenocamellia neuvo valda*). Treated valda oil is a superb local and topical anesthetic for humans, preventing free (pain) nerve endings from activating; valda oil has no known deleterious side effect.

Attempts to grow the valda plant offworld have been invariably unsuccessful, because of the plant's para-symbiotic dependence on a large variety of local micro- and macroorganisms. . . . Attempts to manufacture valda oil via recombinant technologies have proved financially uncompetitive with the natural product. . . .

Due to the characteristic desire of the Elwereans for privacy in virtually all matters, Oroga's trade surplus is not generally known, but is believed to be in excess of one billion Thousand Worlds Credit Units per Earth year, perhaps greatly so.

Careful investment of the trade surplus by the Cortes Generale, the Elwerean parliament, may add significantly to that sum. . . .

CHAPTER ONE:

"We have to. . . ."

"Anything, David?" Little Marie looked up at me, shuffling her bare feet on the sand. Idly, she picked up a small pebble with her toes, then flipped it waist-high, catching it in a chubby hand.

Marie was better at most manipulations than I was. Put it down to inborn talent; I'd had ten more years to work on my skills. One-Hand said that the difference between the two of us was a strong point in favor of heredity over environment.

Whatever that meant. I guess he was talking about my Elwerie father. He didn't know who my mother was. Some lower, of course. We didn't know who either of Marie's parents were, except that they must have been lowers, too.

She let the pebble drop to the ground. "Did you get anything at all?"

I shrugged. "Just a little. Too damn little." I patted my tunic just above the waist, where I'd stashed the purse I'd lifted off the tipsy Randian trader coming out of Alfreda's House of Pleasures. "I got a few pesos, a ten-credit tweecie chit."

I didn't tell her about the firestone ring I'd twisted off his finger. I don't know exactly why; I could have trusted Marie. But I was going to add the ring to my

1

cache, and I'd kept that secret, even from her. The ring and the pieces there were just too fine to give to One-Hand. Dammit, the ring was so *pretty*. I couldn't bear the thought of seeing it broken up, the gold melted down, the stone sold separately.

No one in the market paid the two of us any attention. A couple of ragged children weren't unusual in the Lower City markets; we were unnoticeable among the endless rows of ramshackle stalls huddled up against the rainbow walls of Elweré like moss on a tree.

But just because I wasn't noticed, that didn't mean I wasn't noticing. When you're lifting, your eyes are as important as your hands.

Away from the walls, at a stall set up next to the fountain in the center of the square, an overfed merchant haggled with a mannafruit vendor.

Goddam talkative buzhes. They had been going at it since before I'd made my last run. The two could have been arguing about any quantity, from the squeezings of a single fruit to several tonnes. When money was tight in Lower City, every negotiation was protracted.

But maybe, though . . .

I nudged her. "See Arno's stall?"

Marie shot a quick glance without turning her head. "He hasn't taken his hand off his pouch for an hour. It isn't *fair*."

I shook my head and tried to smile tolerantly. "Fair doesn't have anything to do with it. I wish you'd forget you ever heard that word." I glanced down at my left hand, the thumb still swollen and purple from One-Hand's last fit of anger. "And we'd better keep looking, or we're not going to make Carlos' quota today."

"But if we can't make quota—"

"We *have* to make quota."

Across the hot sand of the square, an Elwerie walked through the crowd. He was a youngish one, maybe forty or so—just about my age, perhaps. It was hard to tell; they don't leave Elweré without wearing their masks, and their defensive harnesses mask their normal posture.

But we didn't bother Elweries. Nobody bothered Elweries. Their harnesses' circuits could detect an attempted lift as easily as a potential attack, and the twin autoguns mounted on the harnesses' shoulder pads would treat a lift the same way. You can't argue with or distract a barrage of two-centimeter silcohalcoid projectiles.

While the Elwerie made his way through the crowd, a t'Tant fluttered by overhead. Several of the children around us stopped their endless game of tag long enough to pick up rocks and throw them skyward.

Not that the rocks came close to the low-flying t'Tant; their ability to fly comes only partly from their leathery wings. The rest comes from a levitating ability that was strong enough to fling the rocks back at the t'Tant's would-be tormentors.

One stone went astray. It came near enough to me to trigger my reflexes; I caught it with my left hand. My bruised left hand.

"Damn." *And damn One-Hand, too.*

I shrugged. It was daytime; it wouldn't be dark for a few hours. T'Tant, while gentle, clownish, and distant in the light, turn savage in the dark.

Over at the foot of Joy Street, a schrift walked into the market. People moved quickly out of its way. It was a huge creature, easily twice my height, its gray skin hanging loosely on its massive frame.

Schrift always looked strange to me; their proportions are all wrong. Their forearms and lower legs are disproportionately long; the extra joints in their fingers make their hands look broken.

The schrift's head was almost featureless: no hair or

protuberances, only holes for its ears, and twin slits of
its nasal openings.

And the eyes. The eyes of a schrift always scared me.
They glowed purply, even in the daylight. I wouldn't
have ever wanted to see them in the dark. The mouth
was a horror of teeth, rows and rows of finely pointed
white needles.

"David!"

"Don't even think about it." This schrift wore a massive jewel-inlaid necklace. The gold alone must have
weighed half a kilo. And then there were diamonds,
and a gorgeous firestone—the firestone, all by itself,
would have been worth tens of tweecie chits, hundreds
of Elweré pesos.

"Marie, you never bother a schrift. *Ever.*" Other than
a gray hempcloth breechclout, the necklace was the
schrift's only clothing. But why the breechclout? As I
understood it, even other schrift wouldn't care what
sex it was—why bother? "Remember One-Hand saying
that their reflexes are faster than ours?"

"Yes."

"He wasn't lying that time."

Confidently, she smiled up at me, cocking her head
to one side to flip the hair out of her eyes. "I can take
him, David. Honest."

"*Listen to me,* will you? You can't."

I had to stall, to keep her talking just for a few
moments, until the schrift had made its way through
the market, and had moved out of sight. Marie would
have tried to take it on, more for my sake than for her
own.

"It's an alien, little one. Not like us." I put out a hand
and stroked the fine hair at the back of her neck. If she
tried to run, I could grab her hair.

Maybe I had a half-sister, up in Elweré. Maybe not.
But even if I did, even if I had been legitimate, and

raised as an Elwerie, I couldn't have cared more about her than I did about little Marie. Nobody else ever *trusted* me.

"And you can't distract it," I went on. "Its mind doesn't work the same way ours do. That thing"— I started to point my chin at it, but caught myself— "that thing could pick you up, bite your head off, and set your body down—all before you finished clipping through the chain around its neck. It's got a faster reaction time—so you leave schrift alone. Got it?"

She glared up at me with the petulance of a child who has been told no. "I'm *hungry.* Can we break for a while and get something to eat?"

I looked around the market. There really weren't any likely prospects. Too many of the people were as poor as we were, or worse. And it wasn't worth the risk of hitting on those who didn't have much; not only were they more likely to be on guard, but the payoff was so damn low.

It was all because of the Elweries. *They* called themselves Elwereans, but they were just Elweries to us. They had cut back on hiring lowers, both for work in the valda fields and in Elweré proper.

Add to that Amos van Ingstrand's increased standard bribe for work in Elweré, and the result was trouble in Lower City. Except for Joy Street, damn near all the money in Lower City came from Elweré.

Too little money, of late.

I took a moment to total the day's take, added it to the likely profit from another run or two down Joy Street, and decided that I didn't like the sum. Not at all.

I patted the back of her head. "Carlos is going to beat us if we don't make quota." Which was true. One-Hand accepted no excuses.

Marie frowned, then brightened. "It might be easier to work on a full stomach." She patted herself on the belly. "Really, it might."

I gave up. "It might, at that. Mannafruit?"

She nodded. "Big ones?"

"Sure."

Arno the mannafruit vendor and I had a standing deal: I didn't hit on his customers until the victim was well away from the stall, and he would sell me small quantities of mannafruit at cost.

We both cheated, of course; that's the way things worked in Lower City. I had no way of knowing what Arno's cost really was, and Arno didn't know about Marie. I had no intention of telling him.

"All right, little one. Meet me at the foot of Joy Street—we'll try to work some offworlders. But don't you start until I get there."

She nodded, her small face almost glowing as she smiled up at me. "I know I could take an offworlder or two, if I had a little food." She emptied a pitiful handful of coins from her inside pocket and dumped them in my hands. "Don't spend it all."

"Will you please get going?"

She left, scurrying across the sand-strewn stones like a lizard running for cover.

I kept my distance from the buzh at Arno's stall, going so far as to stand on the customer's left side, ignoring the purse on the other side of his robes.

Finally, Arno wiped his hand on his apron and stuck it at the buzh. "A fair deal. I'll deliver tonight."

As the merchant left, I moved over in front of Arno and rested my elbows on the counter, propping my chin in my palms. "Really, Arno—a fair deal?"

Arno nodded solemnly, wiping a few beads of sweat from his glistening scalp. "And a reasonable profit,

David, considering the times. How is your business today?"

"Not good. I need a couple of fruit, but I'm a bit short of coin. . . ."

Arno shook his head. "No credit. I'll sell to you at cost, but that's the best I can do. Business isn't all *that* good."

"But people still need to eat."

"True. I do manage to sell a fruit or two, here and there."

"Arno, you would sell your w—" I caught myself. Rumor had it that Arno had been forced to sell his last wife to a valda planter.

As the mannafruit vendor angrily belted his apron tighter around his waist, I kept my eyes off the box of fruit on the rough wooden counter, each juicy yellowish sphere half the size of my head.

"Look," I said. "We have a deal. I left him alone. I didn't—"

"Pfah. You couldn't. He isn't the sort to be distracted. He kept his hand on his pouch the whole time he was here. And as far as our deal goes, I *could* turn you in to van Ingstrand's Protective Society. I'm supposed to get something for my taxes."

I smiled. I had him now. "And if I told him how you've been cheating on your percentage? If I showed him facts and figures to prove it?"

"You couldn't—"

"Are you sure, Arno?"

"Three pesos."

I shrugged. "Fair enough." The three pesos wouldn't make enough difference anyway. Marie and I would have to have almost a record afternoon now if we were to avoid One-Hand's fist.

I dug my right hand into my tunic and pulled out

three copper coins. "But the fruit had better be big, Arno. And fresh."

As I handed over the coins, Arno grasped my wrist for a moment, visibly thought better of it, then let go. Just as well—for Arno: I'd already retrieved my blade with my right hand. Another second, and Arno would have been missing a few tendons.

"Sorry, David." He *tsk*ed. "I just wanted to see how bad it is. He's been beating you again."

"He's scared, Arno. And so am I. Things are tight."

"But your *hand*." Arno shook his head, slowly. "It has to slow you down. And that can't be any good."

It did, but I didn't want Arno to know that. So what if he sounded sympathetic? In Lower City, sympathy could turn vicious, without the slightest warning.

"Try me." I settled my blade more firmly between the middle and right fingers of my right hand. It was practically invisible, but one swipe could open his throat. "Just you try me, Arno."

He ignored the threat. "Why do you stay with him, David? Why? If you need money, I could use some help around here."

It was none of Arno's business, and besides, I really couldn't have answered. I didn't even know the answer. Maybe it was because Carlos One-Hand was the closest thing to a parent that I'd ever had, that I could remember. Maybe it was out of fear of what the old man would do to Marie if I wasn't around. And maybe it was that One-Hand and Marie were the only stable things in my life.

Maybe, maybe, maybe. "Just give me the fruit."

"That's *good*." Marie peeled back more of the thick yellow skin and took another bite of the purple pulp below, using her free hand to wipe the dripping juice off her chin and into her mouth.

"Not so fast," I said. As though I should criticize. I'd already eaten mine on the way over, and taken several longing looks at hers. "Make it last." I leaned back against the wall of a house at the foot of Joy Street.

Joy Street was a mixture of hard-bitten business establishments and fantasy—the fantasy carefully preserved for the advantage of the hard-bitten business establishments. Little of it was for the benefit of lowers; few in Lower City could afford the coin for professionally supplied exotic pleasures.

That made it hard to work. Since only Elweries and offworlders could afford most of Joy Street, both Marie and I would be out of place, and noteworthy.

But at the foot of the street, the facade crumbled. Just a bit: the two-story stone buildings didn't look as clean; the beckoning holos sometimes flickered and went out.

"Some possibilities ahead." Marie took a final bite of her fruit, licked at the inside of the skin, and dropped it to the dirt.

I looked up. Coming down the worn steps of a marble building, under a strobing holo proclaiming that it was THE HOUSE OF ALL PLEASURE, were three men in the blue-and-silver uniforms of the Thousand Worlds Commerce Department. All looked sated; the tall, chubby inspector in the middle was positively weaving, the two others taking turns supporting him down the steps.

I considered it for a moment. "They could have been picked clean."

"No way—they've still got their rings."

Well, maybe they had some coin. It was worth a try, at least. "How do you think we should play them?" I'd already decided that, but Marie liked the illusion of having a choice. I guess we all do.

"Silly. Please-help-me, of course. What kind of story do you want to use? Steerer?"

"I'm too ragged." I gestured at my tattered, yellowing tunic. Which was really too bad. In a more prosperous time, I could have pretended to be a steerer for one of the houses, and picked their pockets, lifted their rings, wallets, and knives while supposedly helping them find another place to spend their money. "Nothing fancy. Keep it simple. Just babble—and watch your timing. Don't cut and run until they're focused on me."

I took a deep breath. Damn, but it still didn't get less frightening. There was another side to it, too—lifting was perversely exciting. "Are you all set?"

She unclenched her right hand, just enough to let me see the silvery gleam of the tiny curved blade she held flush between her second and third fingers, only a sliver of the convex edge showing. A thief's blade is not an easy thing to use; it has to be kept almost totally concealed.

"Go ahead." Marie lifted her chin. "I'm not a baby."

I pulled back my hand and gave her a firm slap on the cheek, my palm cupped to maximize noise while minimizing damage.

Screaming in pain and fear, Marie ran toward the three inspectors. "Help me, please—*he's going to hurt me.*"

I paused for a scant heartbeat before running after her. "Come back here, you . . ." I puffed and panted after Marie. Of course, I could have outrun her, but the point of the exercise was to catch up with her *after* she reached the inspectors.

The lead CD inspector didn't quite know what to make of the tattered little girl who ran blindly into him. "What the *hell?*"

He was a big man, and the five hashmarks on his right sleeve made me more than a little nervous. It wasn't impossible that he was experienced enough, salty enough, to pick up on what was happening.

Just be careful, little one, I thought.

I stopped a few feet away from the group, balancing myself on the balls of my feet.

"Give her to me. I'll pull the little bitch's head off."

The big man handed Marie over to the inspector behind him and turned to face me, a puzzled expression on his dark, leathery face.

I had a bad feeling about him; his brown eyes were clear—not glazed. I wondered if he was too strait-laced to sample the more . . . exotic pleasure of the house. And he just might be alert enough to—

Never mind. I suppressed a smile. There was a slit at the bottom of his shirt pocket. Marie had gotten to him already.

"What do you *want* with the child?" The big Inspector planted himself directly between me and the one holding Marie. He set his hands on his hips. "Well?"

That was the way with Terrans. They ran the Thousand Worlds, and the Commerce Department wouldn't interfere with the—hah!—domestic affairs of Oroga. After all, some Elwerie might object to being criticized for the way lowers were systematically excluded from the wealth that valda oil brought in.

And since the Terrans didn't give a damn about lowers as a group, it was ten to one or better that any individual Terran would try to salve his conscience by protecting a frightened little girl.

I didn't feel bitter about it, not at all. After all, this hypocrisy brought in a large portion of my income, didn't it?

"It's none of your concern, Spec. Just hand the girl over. Private matter."

The big man smiled. "I don't *think* so." He stepped to one side, gesturing at Marie with feigned courtesy. "*Unless* you think you can get by me, and take her away from Gene." He shook his head. "*Prob*ably not a good idea."

Cradling Marie in his arms, the fat man held her high against his chest. It must have been a ticklish procedure for her to slip a hand down his chest and slice the bottom of his pocket.

Just a bit more of a stall. . . . "Look, we're all men here."

The third inspector, a small man with slick black hair and narrow, cruel eyes, chuckled. "Listen to the kid— 'We're all men,' he says. *I* am. Just proved it. Five times."

The big man half turned. "Shut up, Stan. Besides, I've talked to the girl you go to. Says you can't make it without being—"

"*That's a lie!*"

"I said to shut *up*." He hitched at the truncheon dangling from the right side of his belt. Just a stick. The Commerce Department doesn't let inspectors take advanced weapons off the reservation anymore, for fear that some lower might make off with one.

"Now, *you*," he said, turning back to me, keeping his hand on the nightstick, "talk to me. Make it *good*."

I spread my hands. "Look. I gave the girl two pesos. She took them and ran off."

The fat one held Marie protectively tighter and glared suspiciously at me. "Whatcha give her the coin for?"

I smiled, forcing myself not to vomit from self-disgust. "Same thing you got in there." I jerked my thumb toward the house. "What else? But we don't have a problem. Just hand her over and—"

The one called Stan took two quick steps forward, spat in my face, and backhanded me to the ground.

Stan was slow. I could have slipped under his arm, snapped my blade into my palm, and opened him from throat to crotch.

But that would have blown the play, and probably caused more trouble than it would have been worth. The Thousand Worlds doesn't take kindly to locals killing even low-ranking inspectors.

On the other hand, blowing the play didn't seem like such a bad thing as I lay in the dirt, pain shooting up and down the left side of my face.

Stan stood over me and toed me in the side. Not hard enough to crack ribs, but not gently, either. "Let me cripple him a little, Gene—goddam little pederast. The girl can't be much more than twelve, maybe thirteen."

Not a bad guess, if he was thinking in those overlong Terran years. But—

"And what good would that do?" Gene sighed, the playful emphasis in his phrasing gone. "The kid's probably as much a victim as the girl. May as well give her a chance to get away, then let him go."

"Please, Gene." He actually growled. "Just let me break a couple of fingers."

Marie should have finished with the fat one by now. Time to get up and work on breaking off. Moving slowly so as not to irritate Stan, I rolled to my knees and brushed at my right sleeve to make sure that my blade was still secure in its sheath.

Ever so slowly, I rose to my feet. "Please. Don't hit me anymore. *Please*." I always did a good grovel.

Stan reached a hand toward my throat.

"*Ow!*" Clutching at his chest, the fat Inspector dropped Marie. Two slim leather wallets and a handful of coins, rings, and flat octagonal keys fell to the ground.

Marie's eyes grew wide; she scrabbled across the ground in a panic.

"Stan—grab him. They're a couple of thieves."

It figured that the big man would work things out first; the fat inspector was still looking down at the blood flowing onto his palm, puzzlement written across his face.

No need for restraint now. I snapped my blade into my palm and slashed across the inside of Stan's right wrist, barely feeling the resistance as I cut through his tendons. Stan wouldn't have much use of that hand for a while.

I kicked him in the knee for good measure as I ducked out of way of his lunging body.

The fat inspector reached for Marie. She ducked, slashed, and ran.

I wasted a precious half-second trying to work out some way to pick up Marie's dropped loot. But there wasn't any way: the big man was drawing his truncheon, already in a catfooted fighting stance.

So I turned and ran, not looking over my shoulder. There was simply no way that a sexually exhausted, more than half-drunk inspector was going to catch me.

And I felt nothing for any of them. If they left the Commerce Department reservation, they deserved what they got.

Marie was waiting for me just outside our usual entrance to the honeycomb of abandoned mineshafts.

It was well away from the heart of Lower City, which kept it reasonably private, and it was huddled up close enough to the mountain Elweré was built on so that I wouldn't have to be bothered by looking at the rainbow walls as I came home. Elweré was always like a ripe, juicy mannafruit, dangling just out of my reach; I preferred to keep it as far out of my reach as I could.

Best of all, I knew where all the boobytraps were in this tunnel—or thought I did. One-Hand and I had placed them ourselves. That was one of his innovations, he said; he claimed he'd started the practice of booby-trapping.

"David," Marie whimpered, as she cringed back against the massive boulder next to the entrance. "I'm sorry." A tear worked its way down through the dust on her cheek. "I would have given—"

"Shh." I smiled down at her, then patted her on the cheek. "Save it for Carlos."

She looked up at me, returning my smile. "You think it'll work?"

"No. But it's worth a try." I considered the setting sun for a moment, then pulled my flash out of my pouch. "We'd better get inside." Even the Elweries didn't come out at night—t'Tant.

The path from the entrance to our home was long and involved, including eleven separate turns and forks.

The trick in the warrens was always to stay on the known path, never venturing off it—no matter what. I knew where to step aside to avoid triggering a deadfall, where to hop over a tripwire or sidestep a mine—but only on the usual path. Stray too far away, and I'd be in someone else's territory. Maybe they placed traps themselves, maybe they didn't—but the only way to find out wasn't worth the risk.

Boobytrapping was an expensive practice, though; I'm sure that not a lot of other warren dwellers did it. In more prosperous times, Carlos had shelled out tweecie credits—lots of them—to buy blackmarket plastique at the 'port.

Laying them down was an art. The idea was to put what Carlos called "attention getters" far out along our path, with the more deadly traps closer to home. We didn't want to have a lot of bodies clogging the tunnels; we just wanted to be left alone.

I didn't know how many other lowers lived in the mines. Easily several thousand, though—some of them other thieves who also needed the security and privacy of a hidden home, some escaped valda fieldhands who lived near the exits at night, sealing the holes with stones and brush to try to keep out the t'Tant.

As we arrived at the pile of rubble that blocked off our home from the rest of its shaft, I gestured at Marie to precede me, then stashed the firestone ring under a mine hidden in the heap, and clambered over the pile, following her.

One-Hand was swearing to himself. He'd been doing that a lot lately. He paced back and forth, rubbing the stump of his left arm with his hand, his greasy salt-and-pepper beard half stuck in his mouth.

"Well," he said, as he saw us. He hitched at his blue silk tunic. "I see that the two of you have finally decided to come home."

I jumped down onto the soft green everclean carpet—a relic of our better days—and resolved to keep my mouth shut, ignore Carlos' sarcasm. Apparently decrepit as he was, one-handed and all, his reflexes were almost as fast as a schrift's. And his hand was hard.

I emptied my tunic onto the carpet, motioning Marie out of the way.

Carlos stared at me, then at Marie. "What are you holding out?"

"Nothing, Carlos."

"Nothing," Marie echoed. "Just like David said."

One-Hand brushed his hand down the front of his tunic, then took a step toward Marie.

I held up a hand. The bruised one. "It's not her fault, Carlos. I slipped up while cutting a purse." I waved the bruise under his aquiline nose. "My left hand isn't working too well, for some reason." I held out my right hand, as though offering it as a sacrifice. "Go ahead. Hurt this one. Then you can be sure I'll miss quota tomorrow."

Carlos One-Hand shook his head, his limp gray hair whipping around his thin, withered face. "No." He smiled affectionately. "I'm sorry about your hand. You're correct; it's my fault."

He started to turn away, then spun back and hacked down at me with his stump.

That was his way of accepting my excuse. If he had been really angry, he would have used his hand.

I ignored the punches and kicks, as much as possible; his heart didn't seem to be in his work today.

That had to mean something. But what?

Finally, he let me cringe against a rough-hewn wall, and then turned to Marie. "I know why I bother with him. I know why I let him get away with cheating the old man that fed and raised him. When he gets old enough, I'll get him to work Elweré for me. Make me rich, he will. But you—you're only good for one thing—"

"Leave her alone, Carlos." I'd had enough. Besides, he'd tired himself out, pretending to beat me to a pulp.

Speaking up wasn't too much of a risk. I hoped.

"If you didn't have something on your mind, you would have hurt me worse." The night before, he had kicked the hell out of both of us, and just sent us out in the morning.

The old man hesitated for a moment, stroking at his beard, then nodded.

"Quite right." Pulling up a cushion, he dropped to the rug, seating himself tailor-fashion. He crooked his finger at Marie. "You sit down near me. You," he said, beckoning to me, "you can get out of the corner now.

"Listen carefully—I've been thinking this through for a while." One-Hand tugged at his beard. "We're not making enough with the usual slice-and-run, correct?"

I didn't bother to answer.

Marie did. "What else can we *do?*"

"Shh. He'll tell us." I shook my head. Whatever Carlos had in mind, I was sure that it wasn't going to be either safe or pleasant.

"Now," he said, warming to the subject, "I can't send David here into Elweré, at least not yet." He smiled at me. "We've got to put a few pounds and a few more years on you, then get up enough of a stake to set you up like a proper Elwerean."

"Damn Elweries—"

"Elwereans." He punctuated the word with a slap. "That's what they call themselves, and you had better get used to it. I don't want you to use that other word again. When we try to pass you as an Elwerean—"

"Like you used to do?"

"Yes." He waved his stump. "And until I lost my hand, I did very well, for quite a few years; I made a good Elwerean. I stole you out, didn't I?"

"That worked *real* well." I was the last of seven or eight Elwerie—*Elwerean*—infants that One-Hand had kidnapped, then held for ransom. But my father didn't pay; he wanted his bastard dead, not returned. So he had posted rewards for both Carlos and me.

Not dead-or-alive rewards—just dead. Carlos would show me the old fliers, every once in a while.

"It did work well, until . . ." He let his voice trail off.

He'd never told us how he used to get in and out of Elweré. There was always talk among the lowers about the Great Tunnel, which would lead into Elweré, and to food, and warmth, and safety.

Could One-Hand have found the Great Tunnel? I guess it was possible. He couldn't have actually entered as a citizen; the Elwereans could afford the offworld technology to check finger and retina prints. Maybe he had found a way to enter on a work permit, and then leave the prescribed areas and dump his work harness.

Maybe—

"David." A sharp clout brought my attention back to the present. "Pay attention, if you please. What we need is one big haul. We've got to steal something big enough so that we can buy half a tonne of food—and new clothes for you. Then we'll hole up here for a couple of years, and get you ready to take on Elweré."

"Wonderful idea, Carlos," I said sarcastically. "Now all you need to do is find the something big enough, no?"

"How about Amos van Ingstrand's brooch?"

I stood up. "For*get* it."

One-Hand's eyes twinkled as the old man smiled up at me. In his younger days, Carlos must have had a lot of charm. "Just listen. It has seven diamonds. *Seven.* Big ones. How long do you think we could live on what that would bring?"

"About a day. Maybe two."

"We can't," Marie piped up. "He'd find us, Carlos. He'd *find* us."

One-Hand ignored her. "It has to be you. She doesn't have the experience. This sort of thing needs more than fast fingers."

"Right. Try insanity." My hands balled themselves into fists. "You can beat me just as much as you want to—"

"Precisely."

"—but we *can't*. Marie's right. He'd hunt us down, find us."

"How?" One-Hand shrugged.

"Through the fence, maybe? Elren Mac Cormier isn't known for keeping her mouth shut."

"How about Benno the Exchanger? Think about it."

I started to shake my head, then stopped. That began to make sense. Of all the people in Lower City who dealt in stolen and black-market goods, nobody had as much of a reputation for closed-mouthedness as Benno. We'd never dealt with Benno; his prices were awful.

"No, Carlos. It's still too risky. This might be the one time that Benno sells out."

"You know his daughter. You might be able to feel her out," he said, smiling. "Perhaps—"

"Gina keeps away from her father's business. That's why she's in a house on Joy Street. Just think, Carlos— can you imagine the sort of reward van Ingstrand would offer? Stealing the brooch would make him look like a fool."

One-Hand sucked on his lip. "I'll make you a deal. Do it, and after tonight I'll leave her alone . . . at least for a while." He jerked his head toward Marie.

I looked over at Marie, seeing the panic and fear and hope in her face, almost hearing her plead with me. But what was she asking for? A yes—*please, make him leave me alone, David*—or a no—*it's too dangerous*?

"Carlos, the deal is you leave her alone forever. And starting *now*."

He chewed on his lower lip for a moment. "Done."

FIRST INTERLUDE:

Eschteef and the Thief

Eschteef raised its head to look at the setting sun, its inner eyelids automatically sliding over its corneas and then immediately darkening, protecting the retinas from the brightness.

It was getting late. Its blunt fingers took the last pendant from its display hook, placing it with exquisite gentleness in a velvet niche of the massive wooden box. Eschteef was alone at the smallest of the three stalls that the schtann rented from Amos van Ingstrand to display its wares in Lower City—but, in another way, a more real way, Eschteef was never alone.

And it never would be alone, it never could be alone. As it caressed the smoothness of the onyx pendant, Eschteef could feel the cherat, the mindlink with the other members of the schtann, reflecting and amplifying its pleasure at the pendant's simple beauty.

Eschteef reached deep in its mind to feel the deeper cherat, the one with the subtler but richer taste. The schtann was on many worlds, and it had existed for thousands and thousands of years, and would for thousands and thousands more. Dimly, Eschteef could feel cherat with the others of his schtann, some separated by distances so vast that light would take tens of years to span the gap, others separated by time itself.

But the separation didn't matter. The others—the

21

living, the dead, and the yet-to-live—were always with it. Eschteef would never be alone.

It is time to close shop for the day, it thought, not without a trace of regret.

Even though few of the humans in the Lower City could afford its wares, there was sufficient reward in watching them admire its work. And there was profit to be made from the Elwereans. And pleasure there, too.

Not the same sort of pleasure that cherat with the others provided, of course, but that was to be expected; humans were not part of the schtann, and the mindlink was absent.

Still, there was a certain something in watching a human's eyes widen, or seeing it draw in a sharp breath at the sudden display of a particularly good piece of work.

Such faces these humans had! Even after twenty years on Oroga—real Schriftalt years, not these flitteringly short Orogan ones—those faces still caused Eschteef to feel wonder. And pity. Forever denied the true communication of cherat, humans had to make do with facial muscles as a way of sharing feelings. The poor crippled creatures . . .

That is not fair, it thought, chiding itself for its insensitivity and pride. Being born a schrift and having become a member of the metal-and-jewel-workers' schtann had been Eschteef's destiny, and its good luck; it was not a reward, just as the humans' individual prisons of their own minds were not their punishments.

I have spent too much time around the Elwereans; I begin to mistake fortune for virtue.

That was one of the least attractive traits of that strange race, the almost universal belief that whatever benefit came one's way was simply a reward for being virtuous. A reward! As though being born wealthy were a reward for the virtue of a creature that hadn't even existed until it had been born.

A dim feeling of coming danger warmed Eschteef's mind. It was Hrotisft, of course, warning all of the oncoming night.

Eschteef hissed in amusement. Hrotisft acted as though Eschteef didn't have eyes in its head. Even after more than a hundred years, Hrotisft tended to treat Eschteef as though it still was the youngling that Hrotisft had brought into the schtann. Hrotisft had brought many younglings into the schtann; it treated all the same way.

That was something that Eschteef envied. There were no breeding ponds on Oroga, no childgrowers. Eschteef would not have the joy of bringing a young one into the schtann for many years, not until it returned to Schriftalt.

The feeling of coming danger grew; Eschteef quelled it with a louder mental hiss. There was still ample time to pack up and be home before dark, before the t'Tant turned savage.

But perhaps Hrotisft was right. Eschteef had a tendency to gather its thoughts with the oncoming night, rather than prepare for it. Best to finish packing up.

Eschteef turned and took its chrostith down from the wide shelf at the back of the booth. A fine piece of work, it was: a seamless silver pitcher, its surface unmarked and unmarred. Not the kind of work that others of the schtann preferred, not the incredibly detailed work of Sthtasfth or the grandiose creations Ysthstht now built for the humans on Earth.

Ysthstht, I do miss you, it thought, as it wrapped the chrostith in a velvet sheet, then put it away in its own box. *It is possible that I will never see you again, that we will never again speak.* Cherat could not carry a structured thought over the kind of distance that separated Oroga's sun from Earth's.

There was a quiet whisper of sound behind Eschteef; Eschteef spun around. As it did, it saw an ankle disappearing under the rear curtains of the stall. The ankle moved with human slowness.

‹So,› Eschteef said, stooping to grasp the ankle and pull the human back into the stall, ‹we have a thief here, keh?›

Hrotisft signaled alarm; Eschteef quelled it with a mental hiss. There was no need for help. Eschteef could handle the situation by itself.

The human, a middle-aged, terrified male, squeaked some gibberish in its own language. Eschteef could understand the language that most humans seemed to use—but there was no need for the effort, not now. This was not a business situation, and there was no trace of empathy with this human, no cherat.

‹But I will not be cruel; that is not my way.› Eschteef emptied the human's tunic of the stolen scraps of silver by the simple expedient of holding the creature upside down and shaking it. Then it turned the human right side up. ‹I am not a cruel person at all. So I will kill you quickly, before I begin to eat you.›

Eschteef grasped the human's hair and pulled the head back, baring the neck for its bite.

It felt no remorse as it ended the thief's life, and then began to dine.

The thief was, after all, not of the schtann.

CHAPTER TWO:

The Theft

I tucked the corners of the blanket under Marie's feet, then passed my hand over the glowplate set into the wall, dimming it to a vague glimmer. Marie buried herself deeper in the blankets, her chest rising and falling slowly. She always slept well, if lightly. The sleep of the relatively innocent, I guess. . . .

I turned; One-Hand had already retrieved a bottle from his winechest; he tucked it under his stump to free his hand, and then picked up the gameboard.

He tossed it to the middle of the carpet. "Let's play chess."

I shook my head. "I don't feel like a game." A wonderful piece of equipment, the gameboard—Carlos had stolen it out of Elweré long ago, even before me—but I wasn't in the mood to play. "Some other time."

I didn't bother keeping my voice low; Marie could sleep through loud talk, as long as it was a familiar voice, though she would wake at the merest touch or any strange sound.

"You're too keyed up to sleep. A game will be good for you. Sit." One-Hand seated himself tailor-fashion. "Board on. Standard chess."

As I seated myself across from him, the board came

25

alive, casting his face into wicked shadow as the squares flickered from white to black.

The chessmen shimmered into being, then milled around the middle of the board. The knights squared off and ran through the Grand Salute. With raised arms and scowls, the queens and bishops harangued each other, while the rooks just stood still, looking bored. The pawns took tentative punches at each other; the two kings stood with their arms crossed over their chests, looking up at us, waiting for us to choose sides.

"White," he said.

The board stopped flickering. The chessmen sorted themselves out, the white pieces taking their places on his side of the board, the black ones on mine. One-Hand thumbed the winebottle open, took a long drink, then offered me the bottle.

"No thanks, Carlos." That was a familiar opening gambit, no matter what the game. "When was the last time I let you get me drunk?"

"Pawn to king four." One-Hand pronounced the words slowly, carefully; the holographic image of a rough-clad serf responded, shuffling forward two squares. "It has been a while. But it was pleasant, as I recall."

"For you." *Bastard.* "Pawn to queen bishop four," I said.

"You're in the mood for a Sicilian, eh? Very well— knight to king bishop three."

"Pawn to queen three. Looks like a Sicilian, no?" I preferred the Sicilian to the other common king's pawn openings; One-Hand knew the Ruy Lopez, the Stern Wall, and the Giuoco Piano too well.

But my mind wasn't really on the game. There was something strange about Carlos' manner, as though in offering me a deal for stealing the brooch instead of beating the agreement out of me, some measure of power had been transferred from him to me.

"Pawn to queen four," he said. "Relax a little, David. Just think of it as a typical bit of slash-and-run, with an added diversion—you've got to take out his guards. It may be a bit trickier than usual, but not much."

"Pawn takes pawn." My serf crossed to the square holding Carlos' pawn, reached out for Carlos' pawn's throat, then throttled it to death, tossing the body aside. The captured pawn vanished. "That's easy for you to say. You're not the one whose head is going on the block."

"Knight takes pawn." His knight lunged forward and across, drew its sword, and lopping off my pawn's head. "Perhaps . . . but take my word for it—anyone can be taken."

"Knight to king bishop three. And that's nonsense." My king's knight leaped out, waving its sword threateningly at One-Hand's king's pawn. "Amos van Ingstrand wouldn't have been able to reach the top of the Protective Society if he'd been easy to distract."

The Protective Society was the closest thing Lower and Middle Cities had to a government. Or ever would have: Elweré didn't want the buzhes and lowers getting organized. Van Ingstrand would be backed by Elwerie money, if any real threat rose to challenge his power.

Which was unlikely, in and of itself.

"Knight to queen bishop three." Carlos' knight moved out, defending his pawn. "You're confusing the strategic with the tactical. Anyone can pursue a goal over a number of years—that's easy. But damn few can't be deflected from following a goal for a number of seconds. Amos van Ingstrand isn't one of those few."

"Sure. Knight to bishop three."

"It's true—bishop to king two." Carlos always liked to castle early.

"Pawn to king knight three." So did I, come to think of it.

"Bishop to king three." His hand reached out and caressed my knee.

I shoved it away. "Keep your hand to yourself, Carlos. Bishop to knight two."

"Castle." His blocky rook shuffled over two squares to its left, extending a hand to the king, which moved across the rook's square, huddling protectively close.

"Knight to king knight five." Carlos was better at handling complexities than I was; whenever I played against him, I liked to make a lot of even trades, simplifying the game, as quickly as I could. This way, when Carlos took my queen's knight—attacking my queen—I'd be able to work out a quick exchange of queens.

But he didn't take that knight; he took the other one. "*Bishop* takes knight," Carlos said. His king's bishop slid out, and with a wave of the hand, sent my king's knight sinking hellward, down through the board. He smiled. "As I was saying, *anyone* can be distracted. Including you, David. Your move."

He acted as though he'd just done something clever. It didn't look that way. "Bishop takes bishop," I said with a shrug. "I don't see—"

"Knight takes knight." Carlos smiled. "Count it out. No matter how you play, you'll end up a piece down." He sat back and folded his skinny arms across his chest. "Now, if you play Amos van Ingstrand as well as I just played you, you'll lift his brooch just fine."

I stared at the board. One-Hand was right: I'd been suckered again. No matter how I chose to work the series of exchanges, he would end up a piece ahead.

"All you have to do is keep it simple and elegant," he said. "Don't try to be too clever; just do it by the numbers. Keep your disguise on your face and in your head; plan out your routes. Wait for the right opportunity, then create a distraction, then move in, do it, and get away. Got it?"

I nodded. "Got it."

* * *

As part of my varied education, One-Hand had made me read hundreds of books, some of them on cubes, some off tape—until the projector broke; readers are cheap, projectors are both expensive and bulky; makes them tough to lift—and a few, precious, honest-to-Elweré silcopaper books. His intention was to simulate an Elwerie's education, to make me able to pass.

That would be important, later on, he explained—Elweré can be just as dangerous a place as Lower City.

There were some side effects to Carlos' requiring me to read; for one, I fell in love with reading for its own sake.

One book that stuck with me was Richard Milfrench's *On Safari*. Milfrench took his trips through the Earthside jungles seriously, walking across the plains like one of the tigers he hunted.

That hit close to home; lifting was something like that. When I was making a run, I was a hunter on the prowl, looking for prey. Never mind that the prey usually outweighed me, almost always could outfight me—that added to the fear, but it also added to the thrill.

But this was different.

Normally, my objective was to find a vulnerable merchant or offworlder, or maybe a fieldhand in the city after payday; I'd run a routine, make the hit, and get away. Anyone would do, as long as he or she had something worth lifting. The Lower City markets, the area around the port, and the foot of Joy Street were my hunting grounds; any edible prey would serve.

But now, I was hunting big game. And not just any big game: the biggest. I had to locate Amos van Ingstrand while he was out of his house, then I had to find a time when I could create an opportunity, and then take it.

Imagine Milfrench prowling the jungles, looking for a specific lion, having to pass up plump springboks, wildebeests—even other lions. If he knew where the lion's lair was, he would wait there, hoping to shoot it when it came out. If it came out, if it didn't surprise him first, if . . .

Make it worse. Assume that instead of shooting the lion with his rifle, his goal was to sneak up on the lion and touch its tail, without the lion's ever knowing.

Now, you've got the idea. He'd spend most of his time setting up, watching and waiting, preparing for the opportunity, and only a few seconds in tweaking the lion's tail.

It took me forty days to set the lift up, and five seconds to do it. And though I didn't know it at the time, those five seconds changed everything.

I've always wondered, if I knew then what would happen because I lifted that brooch, would I have done it? *Could* I have done it?

I really don't know, not even now. I didn't really care; I couldn't care.

Not then.

I worked my way through the crowd around the baker's stall, heading over toward the jeweler's stall, running down my mental checklist.

One: decide on the mark. I could have skipped that step; but any craft is a matter of attention to details—I was after the brooch pinned to the van Ingstrand's robes, over his heart.

Target, check.

The fat man was already distracted, haggling with the schrift jeweler over the cost of some bauble or other. Always liked jewelry, Van did. But a more thorough distraction would be handy; I thumbed the pseudoflesh-wrapped concussior that I held in the hollow of my left hand. Maybe it was a waste of expensive pseudoflesh, but it did keep the black cube almost invisible.

Two: decide on primary escape route. After I made the lift, I'd work around behind Van and his guards, then disappear in the rush. Simple escape routines are always the best; a close-to-perfect lift is the one where the mark doesn't know it happened until much later. A perfect lift is where the mark never knows, but I've never run into an opportunity for one of those, although Carlos claimed that he had, on more than one occasion.

Primary route, check.

Three: decide on secondary escape route. Again, it could have been argued that there was no real need for this one; if either Van or any one of his three massive guards spotted me, running would only delay the inevitable.

Then again, a thief lives by delaying the inevitable. I shrugged; I could slide under the jeweler's table, then crawl on my belly behind the stall, and make my getaway, shedding my tunic, peeling off the pseudoflesh, and stripping down to my breechclout. Add a bit of dirt, and I wouldn't look at all as I now did.

Secondary route, check.

Four: check the disguise. The physical parts of the disguise were already set, by the time I left home. My face was well shaved and my hair was freshly cut. Makeup under my eyes hid the dark hollows; the cut of my tunic and a scant ounce of pseudoflesh under my chin made me look just a tad overweight.

I looked for all the worlds like a half-rich buzh's son, out for some shopping.

But the mental parts of the disguise are just as important as the physical ones. If I'd dressed the part but didn't act the part, I'd look like a lower in costume; a buzh doesn't walk like the rest of us lowers; more pride, a bit more anxiety—those with less to worry about worry more—and a lot less fear.

So I straightened out of my natural quarter-crouch, threw my shoulders back, and shifted my weight to my heels as I walked closer, staring at the pieces arrayed under the plexi sheath in front of the massive schrift.

Disguise, check.

The staring was supposed to be part of the disguise, but it quickly became more when my eyes caught the pitcher, sitting in a wallmount above and behind the schrift.

That's all it was: a silver pitcher, a third of a meter tall. All of one piece, smoothly curved from its solid base to its narrow lip.

Something came over me; my breath caught in my chest.

The pitcher was so beautiful that I could have cried. Seamless and wonderful, its highly burnished surface caught and caressed the daylight. My hands started to reach out for it, as though it was right in front of me, not separated by two meters.

My eyes misting over, I forced my hands back down to my sides.

The schrift turned away from van Ingstrand to stare at me, its glowing purple eyes boring in. There was no hint of threat in that motion, as though it knew that I could never touch the pitcher for fear my fingers might mar its perfect surface. I wouldn't have done that, not for anything.

"It iss my chrostith, young human," the schrift said, its voice a basso rumble. "My . . . master-work-so-far. It is not for sale."

Nodding, I tore my eyes away. I was supposed to be stealing Van's brooch, not fawning over silver. I couldn't

nderstand it; how could that pitcher affect me this
ay?

I started to look at it again, but caught myself. Never
ind whether it should or not; the fact was it *did* affect
e, did make me feel ... happy, and joyous, and
adequate, all at the same time. Best not to even look
t it, even think about it.

There was, after all, work to do. And this was as
ood an opportunity as I was likely to get. Less than
wo meters away, Amos van Ingstrand was reaching
cross the table for a proffered purse, his huge flipper
f a hand extended.

To his right and behind him, his two blocky body-
uards stood, their eyes on the crowd, their left hands
t their truncheons, their right hands concealed in
ne folds of their cloaks, probably resting on illegal
owerguns.

Five: distract, and go.

I turned as though to leave, dropping my left hand
elow the surface of the schrift's table, and dug my
numb into the pseudoflesh, triggering the concussior's
use. I thumb-flicked it above and beyond van Ingstrand's
ulk, then smoothly continued my turn before closing
ny eyes tightly, opening my mouth to protect my ear-
rums against the pressure wave.

Whump!

Brighter than the sun, louder than the roar of shat-
ering timbers, the concussior went off. My ears rang.

As one, the crowd screamed its fury and fear. A
oncussior's explosion usually meant that the Elweries
vere out in force, seeking to avenge some slight or
rong.

The light died quickly; I moved silently amid the
nimpering, milling, dazzled throng until I reached
an Ingstrand's side.

He stared blindly at me, his mouth working soundlessly, his hands clawing at the air. I snapped my blade into my hand, reached up and cut a ragged circle in his robes, catching and stowing the brooch as it dropped.

As I let the stampeding crowd carry me away, the schrift caught my eye. It stood behind its booth, ignoring the shouting as it stared directly at me.

Wait. I didn't hear that; it wasn't a word. Just a feeling.

Six: escape. I ignored the feeling, and ran. If I had my way, I'd never leave the safety of the warrens again. Ever.

Of course, I knew I wouldn't have my way.

CHAPTER THREE:

"Cleverness Should
Be Rewarded"

I spent the next twenty days studying, sleeping . . . and fearing, of course. I thought I'd gotten used to that.

I was wrong.

"David!" Marie hissed. "I hear something."

Sprawled on the carpet, I lifted my head from the reader, then closed my eyes to listen carefully, the pounding of my heart obscuring the sounds from the tunnel.

The sounds were probably Carlos coming home, but it was always best to be safe. I picked up the control box, flicked it to manual, and punched for the test sequence. A light flashed green; if the noise from the tunnel was an intruder trying to get in, I could set off the charges in the rubble with one push of a button. Getting out of the apparent cul-de-sac wouldn't be a problem: long ago, Carlos had excavated an escape tunnel for just that purpose.

It wasn't much of a tunnel, but it didn't have to be. It was for emergencies, not for normal use. Our "back door" was just a half-meter-high burrow through our back wall, coming out twenty meters above the bottom of one of the mine's vertical shafts. We could climb down the rope we kept there and make our get-away. A thief should always have an escape route

"Do you hear me in there?" Carlos called, from the other side of the rubble pile. "It's me."

"Fine." I kept my thumb on the button, and thought about pushing it anyway. Not for the first time, either. But Carlos was the closest thing to a father that I'd ever had. I pulled my thumb off the button.

"You're still the talk of Lower City, little David." Carlos smiled as he clambered down the pile of rubble, lowering his rucksack to the carpet. "Doesn't matter; they still don't know who you are. Rumor is that some buzh boy lifted it; the buzhes are getting very nervous when the Protective Society makes its rounds."

"No hint that it might not have been a buzh?"

He shrugged. "Not that I've heard. Nobody seems to think that a lower would have the nerve."

"That's good," I said, as sincerely as I've ever said anything. I tossed him the control box.

He caught it, thumbed it back to passive, then armed the pressure detectors, ran through the test sequence, and set it down next to where I lay sprawled on the carpet, one pillow behind my head, the other raising my feet.

"How's the studying coming?" he asked.

"The same." I turned the reader off and pushed it off my lap, letting it fall to the carpet, then closed my eyes and rubbed at my aching temples. "Is all this nonsense really necessary?"

"Good question." He chuckled thinly. "And I've got a good question for *you*: do you really want to get a sword through your belly when you work Elweré?"

"No."

"Then study."

I sighed. If there is anything duller than that Earthie sociologist's discussion of the finer points of Elwerie protocols and manners, I hope I never run into it. Maybe it wasn't totally Dr. Esquela's fault; with all their work done for them by machines, lowers, and buzhes, I guess the Elweries don't have anything better to do than play their endless games, the occasional wound or death providing a bit of diversion and spice.

Still, I don't think I'd want to let Hernando Esquela totally off the hook; he even made the Elweries' Code Duello boring.

Which surprised me. Put it down to a deprived childhood; I never thought that rituals often resulting in sudden, violent death could be made dull.

The only bright spot in the whole book was the posthumous epilogue. Seemed that Esquela had returned to Oroga to do a follow-up study; he'd managed to offend an Elwerie and ended up skewered on a dueling sword.

I often fantasized taking the cube out of the reader and grinding it under my heel instead of replacing it in the library. But Carlos said that *Death and Decadence Among the Elwereans* was a must-read, if I ever was going to work Elweré. Passing isn't just a matter of wearing the right tunic and carrying the right pouch; the internal disguise is just as important.

"No matter what you say about Elweré, this book is slow," I said. "And about as useful as—"

"It will be useful, so keep at it." He shrugged. Carlos One-Hand couldn't have cared less whether or not the book bored me. "The work is necessary. You'll study it, or else." Carlos didn't bother to raise his hand; he knew that I knew what "or else" meant.

"I'm going to take a break." Ignoring his glare, I rose and walked over to the corner of the room. Marie sat there, playing slapjack with the gameboard. She gestured over her half of the phantom pack of cards; an image of a card flipped over, landing square on the thin stack in the middle of the board. It was the three of diamonds.

"My flip," the board announced.

A ghostly hand reached out and flipped over the queen of clubs, snickering mechanically as Marie reached out a hand, then drew it back.

She gestured; another one of her cards flipped. Eight of hearts.

The board flipped over the jack of spades, then barely beat her little hand's snaking strike.

"I win," the board said, taking the stack of cards in the center. "Your flip."

I seated myself opposite the board from her. "How about some checkers? Or Go?"

"I'm even worse at go than you are. Checkers." She glared down at the board. "But give me a minute, please? I want to win first. At least once."

I glanced at the readout above the amber indicator light and smiled; there was no way she could win, not with the board's electronic reflexes set to play slightly faster than was humanly possible. Still, it was good training for hand-eye coordination.

Carlos selected a muslin bag from the pile and dumped its contents on the carpet. "Look, you two, I've brought some more treats home." He tossed each of us a plastic pouch of beef. "Dinner."

Wordlessly, I caught my pouch, snapping my blade into my palm to slice it open while Marie rummaged in a cabinet for a knife.

He glared at me, but didn't say anything. Surprising; I wasn't supposed to use the blade for anything except lifting and self-defense. I wondered how much he'd let me rattle the bars of my cage before reminding me that it was a cage.

With two fingers, I slid out a cube of meat, letting it

grow almost too hot to hold before popping it into my mouth. It was good beef, hot and juicy.

"Nice," I said. I guestured at Marie to open her bag. She shook her head. "I want to finish first."

Carlos dipped into the pile on the carpet and picked up a plexi bottle. "Vitamins—got a good buy on C. And there's some new clothes."

"Mmm." I took a closer look at the pile. A segren spun-glass tunic—no doubt cut to exactly the size I was supposed to be, after I was sufficiently fattened up—a white-and-gold-painted bone full-face casque, an Elwerean pouch, a silver smallsword in a black leather sheath . . .

It was starting to look as though Carlos thought I was ready to take on Elweré. A lot he knew.

But how?

Getting in as a laborer or a buzh wouldn't have been hard, but Elweré was well protected against any thieving or mischief by either. Clamped into a worker's harness, it would be hard to get around unnoticed; computer security systems aren't easily distracted. Getting in as a worker wouldn't be the problem; lifting anything after getting in that way seemed impossible.

Getting into Elweré as an Elwerie was just the opposite. Once inside the city, I could blend in with the crowd; there wouldn't be a problem filling a pouch with valuables. The problem would be getting inside in the first place; I couldn't pass their fingerprint, blood, and retina checks. How had Carlos done it?

I didn't bother asking; he wouldn't have answered. Besides, there was something else that worried me more. "Carlos?"

"Yes?"

"How much *did* Benno give you for the brooch?"

"That would be telling." He smiled knowingly, as

though to say that I wasn't the only one with a cache in the tunnels. "Enough so that this isn't a problem."

For probably the thousandth time, I tried to work out how much he had gotten.

Depending on how well he had haggled, Carlos had already brought home at least five, maybe six thousand pesos' worth of stuff since the lift. And in the twenty days since the lift, he hadn't stopped, going out almost every day to shop, always coming home with his knapsack full.

He wouldn't spend more than half of what he'd gotten for the brooch, not without stopping to worry about the expense. That just wasn't possible, not for any of us. We had all lived on the edge of starvation far too often to squander that kind of money. A part of it, sure—whenever you do a nice lift, you always splurge a little of the proceeds. But not a lot; never more than half.

So . . . figuring his expenditures as conservatively as possible, Carlos had gotten a dead minimum of ten thousand pesos for the brooch.

That didn't sound right. Figure that the diamonds alone were worth sixty, seventy thousand pesos, wholesale. Cut—and to be on the safe side, Benno would be sure to cut the stones—they'd be worth about twenty-five percent less. Benno would pay, say, between ten and twenty percent of the wholesale price of the merchandise. Exchangers aren't known for their generosity. Probably six, perhaps seven thousand was the limit of what Benno the Exchanger would pay for something as hot as van Ingstrand's brooch.

Unless Benno was getting soft in his old age. Which seemed manifestly unlikely.

Carlos toed me in the side. "Get back to work."

I turned the reader back on, but the thought stayed with me. "Carlos?"

"Yes." He wiped beef juices from his chin, then washed down another mouthful with a swig from the winebottle.

"Who did you really sell it to?" Making a loose accusation is an old trick, but sometimes it works.

It didn't, this time. "I don't know what you're talking about—oh. The brooch, again. I sold it to Benno. Just as I told you."

"Benno doesn't pay this well. He wouldn't have given you even ten thousand pesos for it, and you've spent close to that already." Well, I wasn't restricted to my best guess as to what Carlos had really spent, not when I was trying to anger him into being honest.

But he didn't argue with me. He just shrugged. "Get back to your studying, or I'll send you out to work."

I stood. "I'm leaving. Now."

Marie looked up at me, her eyes wide. "But where?"

"I don't know. But I'm beginning to think that Carlos hawked the brooch in the markets. I don't want to be around here when old Amos shows up to take it out in skin."

Carlos backhanded me to the floor. "You're being stupid." He kicked me in the head, sending sparks jumping behind my eyes. "I never tolerate stupidity. Go ahead; leave. Your father still has a reward out for you; I'll let him know who you are, help him find you. Elwereans don't want to be reminded of their little bastards. It's embarrassing; they don't like to admit to being with lower women."

I rubbed the side of my head. "*How?* You're going to let him know that you took his little bastard out of Elweré? You'd dare to do that directly? Or will you really use Benno this time?"

"If I have to for once, I—" A thin smile spread across his lined face. "Very nice, little David. Very clever." He nodded. "Agreed: I didn't sell the brooch to Benno. I used Elren Mac Cormier, instead. She pays better. Much better."

And Elren's mouth leaks like a sieve. That was the word in Lower City. For something taken off an offworlder, go to Elren Mac Cormier—for something hot, don't.

But maybe not this time; maybe, for once, Elren wouldn't let the whole world know about her prize.

"Very clever," he repeated. "And cleverness should be rewarded." He picked up a switch.

I snapped my blade into the palm of my hand.

One flick of the switch, and it fell from my stinging fingers.

"Cleverness should be rewarded," he said, testing the switch against his stump. "At length."

INTERLUDE TWO:

Van Ingstrand and the Guard

With a deep sigh, Amos van Ingstrand straightened himself and stretched broadly. As he did, he reached up, past the overhead mirror, and turned up the exhaust fan to clear the room of the stench.

The fan hummed loudly. He sighed again. Things had gone much too quickly with the second of the bodyguards that had let the boy get away with his brooch. The first one had lasted for days. . . .

Patting Owen's bloody remains, he shook his head. "Too much, Mikos, too much. Terminal shock. . . . You must be careful with the open face. I know you like working on the trigeminal nerve, but . . . just be more conservative next time, more reserved."

Mikos shrugged. "Sorry, sir. I thought he could take it. The first one handled it just fine. *Damn.*"

The ferret-faced little man gave the wide-eyed corpse a token slap, then gathered his tools in his arms, laying them gently in the washer. "Maybe we should use more valda next time?" he asked, one eyebrow raised. He poured in a measured cupful of detergent, then closed the washer and punched the start button with his elbow, careful not to drip blood on the machine's gleaming exterior. "Or a bit of amphetamine, perhaps? It might keep the next one going longer," Mikos said, as he walked over to his sink and began washing himself.

"The trouble with valda oil is that it conceals shock; it

doesn't prevent it. And while I do enjoy opening up the face for the subject to see," van Ingstrand said, tapping at the overhead mirror, "too much valda oil, and what do we have?" He shrugged. "Clumsy surgery, not art."

"It would be pointless, at that."

"So, you must be more careful next time." Van Ingstrand smiled, taking some of the sting out of his words. "*We* must be more careful next time." With one last regretful glance at the body now pointlessly strapped to the operating table, he shrugged out of his blood-spattered robes and his sandals, then padded naked over to the sink, turned the creaking faucet, picked up a fresh cake of white soap, and began to wash himself in the tepid water.

He enjoyed the way the foam worked itself into a pink lather. Amos van Ingstrand was always careful to wash himself thoroughly after a session; it was important to get all of the blood off, to avoid itching later on.

By the time he had finished cleaning himself, Mikos was standing behind him, a fresh robe ready. With a smile of consolation, he helped van Ingstrand into the robe.

A good man, Mikos. One who understood his position, and the realities of van Ingstrand's hobby. After assisting in a failed session, any of van Ingstrand's other men would either be shaking in his sandals or forcing himself not to, fearing van Ingstrand's anger.

Not Mikos. Mikos was an aficionado, like van Ingstrand himself. An artist, in his own little way. Mikos knew that van Ingstrand understood that taking a subject to the edge of pain might push the subject over the edge, and into death. It wasn't always avoidable. In the long run, of course, it wasn't avoidable. But it shouldn't have happened this quickly.

"We'll have to be careful when we find the boy who stole my brooch," van Ingstrand said, still uncomfortable at the absence of its weight from the right side of his chest. "I'll want him to last a good long time." He walked to the door and thumbed the annunciator mounted on the wall.

"Sir," the metallic voice said.

"We are finished in here. Have the body removed, and put the tools back in their place as soon as the wash cycle is finished."

"Yes, sir."

Mikos frowned at that.

"What is it?" van Ingstrand said. "Please."

The other's face wrinkled. "I'd . . . really rather I put away my own equipment from now on. There's a scratch on my tickler, and I know that *I* didn't put it there. I don't mean to accuse anyone, but . . ."

"Very well." But Mikos was still frowning, still upset at how easily Owen had died. Mikos understood how angry van Ingstrand had been, and felt guilty at not restraining himself, giving van Ingstrand less time with Owen than he should have had.

A bit more consolation was called for. "I'll help you," van Ingstrand said.

Mikos opened his mouth as though to protest, then closed it, accepting the gesture as intended. "Thank you. It will take a few more minutes for the cycle to complete itself."

"I know. What are your plans for this evening?" van Ingstrand asked, just to make conversation.

Mikos shrugged. "I didn't think that I'd be free tonight."

"Neither did I." Van Ingstrand thought about it for a moment. Well, there were the payment records to update, and the money shipment to Eurobank to count and seal. Those were tasks that he didn't leave to his clerks, no matter how much they feared him.

But those could wait for a few days. And there was little other business he could do at night. It might be better to decide on some diversion, instead of working.

Normally, he'd be tempted to hire a woman for the evening, but an unsuccessful session in the basement took the spice from that idea. "Perhaps a screening. I haven't have a good screening for a long time."

"Holos?" Mikos brightened. "I like holos."

Van Ingstrand nodded. "I received a new shipment from Earth just last year, but I haven't had the chance to look at much of it. Metro Goldwyn Warner has that new process. Have you heard about it?"

"No—new process?"

"Yes. They take classic flat films, then run them through a computer which . . ." His hands gestured aimlessly. He wasn't really sure of the process. "It reanimates them, as holos. I've only seen a few of them, but *I* can't tell the difference between these and real holos."

"Really." Mikos was impressed. "Did they do that with *Birth of a Nation*? Or *Animus*? That would be so nice."

"Yes. I have those. But I think I'd like to screen the Star Wars series. That would be fun in holo, no?"

"I've always liked it in flat. Those four films are classics."

"Then that's what we'll do." He thumbed the annunciator again. "Screening tonight—we'll start an hour before sundown. The Star Wars films. In sequence, please."

"Of course, sir."

"And I won't want to be interrupted."

"No interruptions, sir."

"Unless someone locates the boy who stole my brooch."

"Yes, sir."

Amos van Ingstrand rubbed his hands together.

That would be worth interrupting the screening for.

CHAPTER FOUR:

"That Will Be Ten Pesos. Now."

My back had pretty much healed over, a few days later, when Carlos sent us out to work Lower City again. "If you don't appreciate sitting around on your lazy ass while I go out and get supplies, you might as well make some money," he had said.

Actually, getting out suited me. Even a permanent state of fear doesn't prevent creeping claustrophobia; I'd been going a bit stir-crazy.

As we exited the tunnels, both of us squinting in the bright sunlight, Marie smiled up at me. "What sort of stuff do you want to do today, David?"

I hitched at my shoulderbag. "Not we. Not today."

For one thing, the area I wanted to go to was near the seedie reservation, and it wouldn't be safe for the two of us to be seen together there; Marie's and my descriptions were probably still circulating well around there, after that fiasco with the three inspectors.

For another, I could run faster by myself, if it came to that—and while I had no particular reason to doubt Carlos' assurances that nobody suspected the identity of the boy who had stolen van Ingstrand's brooch, taking Carlos One-Hand at his word would be incredibly stupid.

"You don't want to work with me anymore?" She

looked as if she was about to cry; I reached out and ran my fingers through her hair.

"No, little one, it's not that. This is just for today. I'll head down into Middle City, toward the port. You head into the markets. Don't be stupid, but do be lazy. With all the money we've got these days, Carlos probably won't beat us, as long we come back with something. Just take the easy ones."

She sniffed. "You talk like I don't know the sharp edge of a blade from the dull one."

I wasn't too worried. Even if she slipped up, most suckers would let her go, rather than turn a cute little girl over to the Protective Society. "Get going; I'll meet you here just before sundown, if I can. If I'm late, wait for me about halfway down the path. I'll be in before it gets dark enough for t'Tant to be a problem."

"What are you up to?"

"I told you: I'm going to work around the 'port."

She sniffed. "Oh. Her."

"It has been a while since I've seen Gina."

"But you'll get some money, too?"

" 'Course. Get going, and—"

"I know. And be careful." She jogged away toward the markets, her feet kicking up sand.

There was another, more important reason that I wanted to be on my own for a while. Gina was only the minor one.

For Gina, I'd need to make some money. But I could take care of the major one without any.

I fondled the firestone ring I'd reclaimed from my stash. With a bit of luck, I'd end up making some money.

So I pulled a makeup kit, a new buzh tunic, and sandals out of my shoulderbag, stuck my makeup mirror on the boulder, and started putting on the color and pseudoflesh.

* * *

The sign outside the third in the row of low stone buildings at the edge of the port preserve read:

ELREN MAC CORMIER, EXCHANGER
Fast Cash   Currency Conversion   Friendly Treatment
BEST RATES IN THE CITY
Our Motto:
"If someone else says that he can do better by you, *he lies*."

It's always a bit tricky to work around an exchanger's place, and not usually a good idea. Exchangers and lifters are partners, at least in one sense; we eat from the same table. It's not polite—and it's always risky—to work where you eat.

But I knew Elren Mac Cormier only by reputation and by sight; we'd never done business directly.

Worth the risk, as long as I could keep the disguise up.

I ducked into the alley next to the building to adjust my makeup and work it out.

Let's see . . . I could carry my age at anywhere from about thirty-five to fifty-five; for this, probably the younger the better.

Thirty-five, then—just into the frustration years of puberty. That felt about right.

I shaved again, digging in the razor over my right cheekbone to add the kind of abrasion that a boy new to shaving might have, then put the razor back in my pouch and took out a half-empty tube of Skintight to remove the worry lines around my eyes. I rubbed more color in below the eyes to get rid of the dark hollows, then added a couple of layers of pseudoflesh to my cheeks—baby fat, they call it.

A bit of oil on my hair, a quick combing, and I was

done. As I examined myself in my mirror, I had to agree that I looked like a buzh, but not like the same one who had stolen van Ingstrand's brooch: I was chubbier and a few years younger.

Good. A bit of nervousness, an occasional stammer, and a pubescent crack in my voice would help, but that wasn't quite enough. I straightened into a buzh's upright posture, then added a solid ten percent of crouch to allow for the nervousness of a boy selling one of his father's rings.

I stashed my makeup kit, my blade, and its sheath in my shoulderbag, stowed the bag under a heap of refuse, and waited quietly for a few minutes while the marks from the sheath's strap faded from my forearm.

As Carlos always said, most of the work is in preparation. Since I wasn't going to steal anything here, there was no need for the blade.

It was just as well that I left it; as I walked through the door, one of Elren's blocky guards frisked me, politely but thoroughly. He led me through a dark foyer into a windowless room, well carpeted, discreetly placed glows providing indirect lighting.

Elren Mac Cormier's office was nicely appointed. The floor was covered by a gorgeous black-and-gold rug. If it was a real Persian, it was probably worth hundreds of tweecies; even if it was a simulacrum, it would still be worth a lot.

The overstuffed visitors' chairs in front of her desk were large and deep, which spoke well for her sense of security—once seated in one of these, it wouldn't be possible to leap out.

The side and rear walls were covered by purple curtains; there could have been no other entrances to the room, or a dozen.

The guard gestured to one of the chairs in front of

her massive, stone-topped desk. "If you will wait here, young sir, the Exchanger will be with you in but a moment."

I took the firestone ring out of my pouch and pretended to fondle it nervously while I waited. There could have been fifty peepholes—there was certainly at least one, although it wasn't necessarily manned right now—and I didn't need to excite any suspicions by searching the room for a safe or cache while I waited.

But there were half a dozen places in this room alone where there could have been a hidden safe, and there was no hint either of boobytraps or of electronic warning devices.

Likely her safe—at least the one where she kept most of her money and her most valuable valuables—was in this room; it's reassuring for an exchanger to do business near the cashbox.

I didn't like the apparent absence of both traps and alarms. I didn't like that at all. There should have been one or the other, depending on whether Elren spent her nights in the building or not.

The absence of alarms had to mean that Elren didn't live here at night. Alarms are only useful if you can go answer them when they go off; since she wouldn't dare go outside to answer an alarm for fear of t'Tant, that indicated that she didn't live here.

So there should be boobytraps.

Unless she took all of her stock home with her? No, that didn't make sense, either; a successful exchanger wouldn't be able to carry a large stock of goods and money home and back every day.

The only thing that left was live guards, supplemented by a safe or two. I suppressed a nod. I should be able to beat live guards and pretty much any lock. And that would be it—assuming, that is, that the brooch was still on the premises.

A large assumption, but one that I didn't have to commit myself to, not yet.

The curtains on the wall opposite me were pushed aside, and Elren Mac Cormier walked into the room. She was a tall, middle-aged woman, with a short, sharp nose and neck-length hair that flipped about her face as she tossed her head nervously.

"Good day, young sir," she said, her calm voice contrasting with her twitchy manner. She smiled. She had good teeth and gold inlays. Exchangers always have good teeth and gold inlays. "I believe we have not done business before. Am I incorrect?"

"N-no," I said, proud of the little stammer. "I've never done this—"

She raised a palm. "Please. Rest easy. Everyone has a first time, for everything." She ducked her head. "And I am both proud and pleased that you have selected me to handle your first exchanging. Is it the ring?" She seated herself behind the desk.

"Ring?"

A note of impatience crept into her voice. "The firestone ring in your hand." Elren Mac Cormier smiled. A young buzh, selling an expensive ring—that looked promising, both for now and for the future. She cocked her head, looking me over from head to foot, trying to decide whether it was drugs or sex.

She would tend to lean toward sex as the explanation: my eyes were clear, and my arms unmarked—and I was nervous enough to suggest that this was my first time.

"Yes. The ring. It's mine," I said, handing it over, "but I don't need it anymore."

"Of course." A little quarter-nod. Sex, she decided.

She donned a loupe and examined the ring carefully, then weighed it on her desk scale. "An adequate firestone, despite the tiny flaw. I can give you four hundred pesos, as gem and gold. Seven hundred, if you'll allow me to sell it openly, as-is."

She kept her smile to herself this time. It was a nice gambit, and she was pleased with herself: a buzh boy, selling a ring he'd stolen from his father, wouldn't want to take the risk of leaving the ring intact, particularly since he wouldn't trust the exchanger's discretion. Not a loosemouth like Elren, if he knew her reputation— not even a legendarily discreet exchanger like Benno, if this was his first time.

I kept my smile to myself, too. Elren wouldn't chop the ring up; that would decrease its value. Which was exactly what I wanted; it was just too pretty.

Still, I had to stay in character. "I'd . . . rather you break it up. It . . . would bother me, if I ever saw the ring on anyone else's finger."

She nodded. "And so it shall be." She looked around the room and grimaced. "I'm sorry, but I don't have my tools here, or I'd pry the gem loose right now, and melt the gold down before your very eyes. I hope you'll trust me?"

"Of c-course," I said, honestly. Of course I knew she wouldn't break up the ring.

She reached down and turned a key, then slid open a desk drawer. A heavy drawer, from the sound of it. That boded well; if the desk was well secured, it probably meant that she kept it locked against pilfering by her guards. Which would mean live guards at night, instead of electronics, confirming my suspicions.

That would be easy to check.

She raised an eyebrow. "I assume you want cash, rather than trade?"

"Y-yes."

"Fine. Are hundreds acceptable?"

I nodded.

She smiled; definitely sex. The Protective Society

frowns on drug traffic among the lowers and buzhes for the same reason it frowns on lifting; drugs also tend to cut down on the take from legitimate business, like foodselling and Joy Street.

So, most drug dealings take place either in Joy Street houses that lowers can't afford, or in hidden corners of Lower City alleyways, the dealer providing the goods, the buyer quickly giving him the exact price, then rushing away—not the sort of situation where you can wait around for change.

On the other hand, Joy Street houses don't mind making change; they're taxed by the Society, just like any other business.

She counted four hundred-peso bills onto the desk, then bid me a good day. "I hope you will return soon," she said. "It has been a pleasure doing business with you."

"That is kind of you to say," I said, straight-faced. Just what I had been thinking.

I tucked the bills into my pouch as I walked out. Now, all I needed was advice. Well, not quite all.

What I really needed was someone to talk to, someone I could trust.

I settled for Gina.

Gina brought a pair of icy-cold glasses of water back to the bed, dew beading their mottled sides. "I should charge you extra for this," she said, as she lay down beside me, propping herself up with pillows. "This isn't an eatery."

Sun spattered through the barred windows and splashed on the bed, her long, so-blond-that-it-was-almost white hair shattering the sunlight into all the colors of the rainbow. She turned over onto her side to sip her water, posing gracefully, one leg folded slightly over the other, the other with toe pointed, accentuating the curve of her thigh and calf. Gina was beautiful. But I guess I'm prejudiced.

"I guess so," I said. "You clearly didn't enjoy yourself." I snorted.

She just smiled, and ran a long fingernail across my chest. "But maybe getting you a drink of water isn't all that much more effort." She set her glass down on the nightstand and curled up next to me, resting her head on my chest. "This cuddling will cost you an extra peso, though."

"Fine."

It was part of a game we always played; we never violated the unwritten rules.

The pretense was that this was always business, that she was just in it for the money. It had always been that way between me and Gina, ever since the day we'd met, several years before, when she'd caught me trying to lift her pouch, quickly doubled me over with a quick kick to the groin, and then offered not to turn me in in return for a half-peso.

Yes, just a half-peso. She could have taken my pouch, which contained more than twenty times that, and turned me in to the Protective Society.

But she hadn't. And any suggestion that she could have made more money off me than she already did was somehow forbidden.

Part of the game. Gina liked playing at it.

Which is why I trusted her now, I guess. If she turned me in for van Ingstrand's reward, she wouldn't have anyone else to play with. Nobody else could have understood her; nobody else would have played.

"I've got a problem," I said. "Give you ten pesos for some good advice."

"How much for bad advice? And how do we decide on the quality—" She caught herself. "Wait a minute— you sound serious."

"Good."

She sat up, draping the top sheet around her shoulders. "You're thinking of leaving Carlos?"

That again. She always managed to bring that up. "No. I wish . . . but I can't." And not only for Marie's sake—although God alone knew what he'd do to her if I left—for my own. "He'd let my real father know who I am. The Elweries—"

"Elwereans."

"*Elweries* don't like to let their bastards live. Even if I had enough money to buy Gate passage, I wouldn't dare. They all have so much money; hunting me down even offplanet wouldn't faze one of them."

"True." She nodded. "So what is it?"

"You remember Amos van Ingstrand's brooch being lifted?"

Her face went pale. "You?"

"Me. Don't look so surprised. I've gotten better since the time you caught me."

She set down her glass and lay. "You'd better have. You know—" She stopped, and went into a feigned fit of coughing.

You know what the reward is, she was going to say. *You know that you're worth at least a hundred thousand pesos to van Ingstrand.* But that would bring up the subject of how much more money she could have made off me, and that the reason that she hadn't was that she cared about me, and that was something she couldn't say.

"—how badly he wants you," she finished, leaving the unspeakable unsaid.

"I know." I pulled her closer to me. *And I know that you won't turn me in,* I thought, wishing that she could read my mind. "Which is why I'm worried. Guess who Carlos took the brooch to?"

She shrugged. "My father's silence is legendary."

It runs in the family, I thought. "And so is his cheapness."

I don't know when or how or why Benno kicked his daughter out; that's another thing I've never been able to bring up. The only hints I ever had were things Gina would mumble in her sleep, the few times that I could get the money and the chance to spend the early morning, the sleeping part of her day, with her. She'd talk to herself in a little-girl voice in her sleep, mumbling promises that she'd be better, if only he'd give her another chance.

"So." She shrugged. "You're safe."

"No. Carlos took it to Elren Mac Cormier."

She was silent for a long minute. "That's bad, no matter how she ends up playing it. Elren doesn't like to break things; she might try to move it offworld."

"Which would be fine."

"Yes, but it's unlikely." She shook her head. "Don't count on it. She's much more likely to sell it back to van Ingstrand, along with some information. Which could be a problem. Carlos was awfully good in his younger days, but one hand makes him conspicuous.

"Then again, the rumor is that old Amos is furious. He might decide to treat her as an accessory, and pry information out of her." She smiled. "And I think Elren is smart enough to work that out. She's likely to let him cool off for a while, even if she decides to go that route. Then she'll talk."

I shrugged. "She couldn't tell him much."

"True. But maybe Carlos' name or description would be enough."

"And maybe Amos wouldn't believe her, maybe he'd decide that she was in on it from the start. He just might—"

"Kill her, just for being involved. That could be very bad."

I shrugged. "Elren Mac Cormier isn't a friend of mine."

"You're missing the point. If Amos touches her, the rest of the exchangers are going to be down on his head. They generate too much money to be trifled with. Collectively, they've got enough to bring in some offworld mercenaries, people good enough to take on the Protective Society. Could be bloody." She sipped her water. "For everyone in Lower and Middle City."

"I don't want that."

"Don't lie to me, David." She stared deeply into my eyes. "You don't really care. You're an emotional cripple—"

"Wait a—"

"It's not your fault, but you're not capable of caring about anyone, anything." She spoke quietly, gently, each word a stab. "You never really had a childhood, did you?"

"Sure, I—"

"How old were you when Carlos first set you to work?"

"Twenty-five, maybe thirty. I don't remember."

She nodded. "That's what I meant. Childhood is when you're supposed to learn a lot of things. Like caring—not stealing. I don't blame you, brought up the way you've been, but you really don't care. Not about anyone."

"That's not true!"

"And does shouting make it true?" Gentle fingers stroked my brow. "Tell me, how would you prevent all this bloodshed?"

I shrugged. "If she doesn't have the brooch, she can't try to sell it to Amos; no reason to take the risk of talking to him, not if she had the brooch, and then lost it."

"So?"

"I'd better steal it, hadn't I?"

She drained the last of her water. "You'd better think that over for a long while. Sounds awfully risky. But . . ."

"Well?"

"Not doing it sounds even riskier. That'll be ten pesos. Now."

"How'd you like to try for eleven?"

She smiled. "I could always use the money."

I met Marie at the mouth of the tunnel. She was sitting cross-legged on a rock, fondling the pouch on her lap, squinting at the setting sun, murmuring to herself.

"Well?" She drummed her heels impatiently against the rock. "How did you do down at the 'port?"

"Not too bad." I tossed her my pouch. "I picked up just short of two hundred pesos, plus a bit of schrift jewelry." That sounded lame. More specific—"A gold beltclip; sold it for another hundred. How about you?"

"Not very well. Only seventeen and a half."

I took my flash out of my pocket and lit it as we entered the tunnel.

"Money is still tight, David, eh?"

"Yes, it is," I answered absently, scanning the floor of the tunnel for tripwires and triggers as we walked homeward.

The problem still was how to handle it. Maybe Elren would just take a sure profit and keep her mouth shut; possibly the whole mess would just blow over. That way, we could go back to Carlos' original plan: hole up, let me continue to study Elwerean behavior, then, when I was ready, start to work Elweré. Just a few runs through Elweré, and I've have enough to last me the rest of my life.

And what then? What do you do when you're rich?

I chuckled. That wasn't a problem I'd ever had.

So, it came down to two choices: either forget trying

to steal the brooch back and hope; or steal it back, hide it, and expect Elren to keep her mouth shut.

But maybe she'd already talked. Or, at least, given out some free hints to Amos van Ingstrand as a foreshadowing of what was to come.

Maybe, maybe, maybe—you can live your whole life on maybes.

"Hold on a second." I stuck my arm out in front of Marie.

I knelt on the floor of the tunnel. This close to home, we set our traps very carefully, hiding them well.

When Carlos and I had set this one, we'd carefully dug a shallow trench for the tripwire, then buried the wire, the charges, and some scrap steel, marking the spot with two pebbles on either side of the buried wire. If anything massing more than thirty or forty kilos stepped on the wire, it would pull the pins from the charges, setting up a loud hissing as the noisy igniters burned away; a scant ten seconds later, the plastique would go off, filling the air with thousands of killing fragments.

This trap was by way of a final, possibly deadly warning; it was intended to announce firmly that proceeding farther was not wise.

The marking pebbles were still there, but they overlapped their own impressions in the dust. I leaned over and dug a finger into the ground. The dirt was too loose; it had been freshly repacked.

Marie looked up at me, her face a ghostly white in the light of my flash. "There's been somebody here."

I nodded. This looked bad. Very bad. Nobody other than ourselves had been in our area of the warrens for years.

"Don't worry about it," I said. "It's nothing."

She considered that for a moment. "No, it isn't. David, you're going to have to do something. Please."

I nodded. "I will. Just give me until the day after tomorrow. Okay?"

She cocked her head to one side. "Okay."

THIRD INTERLUDE:

Miguel Curdova and His Secretary

On the morning of an afternoon, Miguel Ruiz de Curdova always ate little; at noon, he would eat nothing.

It was better to be ravenous after the duel than to risk being logy at the wrong moment during one. Even a first-blood affair could result in death—although that was rare—and second-blood affairs often did. A third-blood affair always resulted in death, of course, even if the seconds had to raise an unconscious loser from the mat and hold him still for the final, fatal thrust.

With, at last count, two third-blood duels to his credit—as well as forty-three second-blood ones, and more first-blood affairs than he could keep track of—Curdova made his preparations with the practiced ease of a bourgeois mechanic.

He toyed for a moment with the remnants of his breakfast kippers, then turned to the delivery box at his elbow and brusquely ordered himself a fresh pot of coffee. Idly, he reached across the Irish-linen table-cloth and picked up an unused silver butterknife, examining his face in its mirror-bright surface.

He was pleased with what he saw. Even after one hundred fifty-eight years of a busy life, his face was only slightly lined, the wrinkles around his eyes much less prominent than the thin dueling scar that curved, snakelike, around his right cheekbone. The dark eyes and thin smile held more than a trace of menace, but no hint of weariness.

Work and exercise, that was the secret. The sheep often remarked how the delegates to the Cortes Generale didn't age properly, and it was true. Busy people didn't have time to grow old. Let the rest of Elweré bask in the wealth that valda brought—somebody had to take the responsibility of seeing that the source of that wealth was properly maintained.

Delegate Miguel Ruiz de Curdova accepted that responsibility as his duty, and his right. He surely could have become Presidente of the Cortes, had he been willing to work toward that, but he preferred membership in three of the more powerful committees.

It was the work that counted, the responsibility. Not the titles. Titles were dross; the work was gold.

The delivery box opened with a quiet hiss; he reached in and pulled out the silver coffeepot. He poured himself a cup, not bothering to notice how the balance of rich Alsatian beans, heavy cream, and Randian sugar suited his palate. If it had been wrong, he would have been furious, but it wasn't in his nature to notice when things went his way; he was too used to that.

He sipped his coffee. Enough dawdling. It was time to get to work. He sighed hypocritically; getting to work pleased him. Lighting his first cigar of the day, he sat back in his chair, drained the cup, then thumbed his phone and raised it to his lips.

"Good morning, senhor," his secretary said. Her voice was a rich contralto, one that should have belonged to a lovely young woman. That amused him. Actually, Doris Reinholt was almost his age, half again his weight, with a face like a pig, and a small mustache.

But she was competent. Which was what counted in a secretary.

"I've a minor affair with Delgado this afternoon," he

said. "Reschedule the meeting of the Trade steering group for this evening. Delgado will likely protest—if he is in any shape to—but do not acknowledge. We'll let Andresen smooth his feathers. The same for Almada; he's getting crotchety in his old age."

"Yes, senhor. I'll inform their secretaries."

"Good. And I'll want those projections on Thellonee's usage. Either the wars are heating up more than the news reports show, or they're stockpiling." If they *were* stockpiling valda oil, that would have to be nipped in the bud. "What is the next major contract coming up for review? Rand?"

"No, senhor. Metzada. The present one terminates at the end of the year."

Metzada was going to be a problem. Damn that Tetsuo Bar-El. . . . "In that case, forget about working through Andresen's secretary. You'd better make an appointment for me with Andresen—dinner, if he's free. Include my sister; he likes her. I'll probably have to straighten him out about Metzada. Again."

Andresen took the Scandinavian part of his heritage too seriously. The time of conflict between the descendants of the Spanish sherry barons and those of the Scandinavian fieldhands was over; now, they were all Elwereans, sharing equally in the wealth that valda oil brought in.

Sentimentality about Shimon Bar-El's world was inappropriate; after all, Shimon the Liberator had been dead for centuries.

But I can straighten him out. "The report from Wells/Puro was due yesterday."

"Mmm . . . just in this morning, senhor. Some problem with the courier—I'll look into it. Do you want me to send the report to you, or will a summary do?"

"Summary, for now." *We'll see*, he thought. No point

in hearing a several-thousand-word pointless report. "No luck, I assume."

"They're sorry to report that there is still no sign of your son. With all due respect for the resources and abilities of Welles/Puro and associated agencies, they—"

"You may delete the honorifics."

"Yes, senhor. Captain T!kau respectfully repeats his recommendation that you terminate the search. He included a new mathematical analysis of the problem; present half-life-to-success is ninety-eight point three Orogan years, at present levels of effort."

"What happens if we double the effort?"

"It won't do much, senhor. Wells/Puro can't—"

"Won't."

"—won't put more agents on the problem. As it is, their Thellonee branch is overloaded. Their estimate on hiring Intertec for a similar effort only brings the half-life down to eighty-nine and a fraction years—and, if I may say so . . ."

"You may."

"I think their analysis is too generous, if anything. No matter how much they open their records, Intertec would still end up spending a lot of time and effort going over the same ground."

"They're doing close to all that's do-able, then."

"Yes, senhor. He does offer another option—to re-open the local search. It's conceivable that the boy is still on Oroga."

"Unlikely. We closed that search more than a decade ago. But he could have been brought back, at least theoretically." No, that would be pointless; the kidnapper wouldn't have dared to keep the boy on Oroga. Too close to Curdova, and his wrath. *My son is of Elwerean blood. Now that he's grown, it wouldn't be possible to conceal him among the fieldhands and lowers. He would stand out.* Still . . . "Tell him I'll take it under advisement."

"Yes, senhor. May I suggest that you begin your morning workout? Senhor Delgado is not your equal with the blade, but . . ."

"But there's no sense in giving him any advantage, eh?" In fact, Delgado's skill with a blade wasn't close to Curdova's. Curdova could handle him easily.

Hmm . . . that might be useful; a bit of embarrassment on the field of honor, perhaps a scar in an awkward place, might teach Fernando Delgado not to drop sneering comments about Miguel Ruiz de Curdova's wasting money in the search for his son.

The search was probably useless, granted. It was almost certain that the kidnapper had killed the boy when Curdova had refused to pay the ransom for the infant's return, all those years ago.

But, perhaps, the kidnapper still lived. For that reason alone Curdova had allowed Amos van Ingstrand to continue as chief of the Protective Society, often throwing support van Ingstrand's way when another delegate advocated putting someone less harsh in. It wasn't necessary that Elweré's main agent in Lower City be a sadistic pig. Simple ruthlessness could keep the lowers and the bourgeois in line; the brutality of Amos van Ingstrand was superfluous.

But I will want a sadistic pig available, if they ever find the bastard who stole the boy, he thought, once again.

Someday, he thought, *someday* . . .

CHAPTER FIVE:

"Make It Stop Hurting. . . ."

It's different on other worlds, but on Oroga, daytime is when you can go outside. Only daytime. Night is a time to stay inside. Because of the t'Tant.

T'Tant are intelligent and gentle during the day, when the plant parts of their brains are enlivened by the sun. They circle in the sky, chirruping merrily, and bask on rocks, always spreading their wings to allow their green upper surfaces maximum exposure to the sunlight. All they need to keep their plant brains happy is sunlight, and, perhaps, the antics of the humans or schrift below to amuse them while they fly.

During the day, they're harmless. They react to an attack by fleeing, or by using their levitating ability to repel the attack. Hurt another creature? Never; that wouldn't be amusing at all.

At night, though, the plant part of the brain shuts down, and the animal takes over.

They turn vicious. They hunt. And while their favorite prey are vrasti, the small, six-legged herbivores that eat both wild and cultivated valda, t'Tant can eat just about anything with blood in its veins. The t'Tant have good digestion.

They're dangerous, but they are an important part

of Oroga's ecology; without the t'Tant, the vrasti would soon eat all the valda plants.

Back when I was younger, when Carlos explained all this to me, I came up with the obvious question: Why didn't the Elweries simply have the vrasti exterminated? That would increase the valda yield—and take care of the t'Tant at the same time.

He referred me to a book on Orogan ecology. It's very complicated, and I don't remember it all, but part of the cycle involves vrasti eating valda, then leaving their droppings in the field, which contain bacteria that attach themselves to the valda plant's roots, a bacterium which helps the valda plant take nutrients from the soil, but which can't survive long outside of the vrasti's gut.

No vrasti would mean no vrasti intestinal bacteria. Which would mean no valda, or, at least, a vastly reduced harvest. The Elweries wouldn't like that.

No t'Tant would result in—temporarily—a lot of very fat vrasti, who could easily finish off millions of dunams of valda fields, which would soon mean no valda.

And the Elweries wouldn't like that, either. Which is why they forbid the killing of t'Tant.

And—during the daylight hours, at least—t'Tant are a sapient species, just like humans, schrift, paraschrift, poncharaire, cetaceans . . . and airybs, if you're willing to stretch a point. Which is why the Thousand Worlds prohibits their slaughter, and why the Thousand Worlds Commerce Department prohibits the import of power weapons onto Oroga. One of the reasons that the Elweries suffer the Protective Society's existence is the unwritten agreement between Elweré and the Society that the Society will keep power weapons out of the hands of the populace.

Muscle-powered projectile weapons—slingshots, bows, crossbows—are allowed; a t'Tant's levitating ability can deflect their projectiles. But the t'Tant's powers aren't great enough to deflect fast-moving bullets or silcohalcoid wires.

Granted, the Commerce Department looks the other way when a case of powerguns, blithely marked FARM MA-CHINERY, arrives for shipment into Elweré itself—after all, the Elweries know where their wealth comes from; their power weapons are used to put down fieldhand uprisings, not kill t'Tant.

But lowers and buzhs are not permitted power-weapons. Which is why we all stay inside at night.

Or, occasionally, wish we could.

I moved quietly through the night, my shoulderbag strapped tightly to my back, my ears primed for the sound of wings flapping through the sky.

I'm sure I looked silly; the nightgoggles that Carlos must have stolen out of Elweré and that I had stolen from Carlos made me look, well, goggle-eyed.

I didn't mind; there was nobody out to see.

Digitized, reduced to the simpleminded on-off pulses of the goggles' circuitry, and then enhanced, displayed on the twin screens, the night had an eerie quality to it, as though all of Lower City glowed from its own light.

Overhead, the stars were bright pinpricks of orange in a pastel-blue sky. That was the way the goggles handled light: the brightest objects were colored red, those of the second magnitude orange or yellow, all the way down to a deep, rich blue that indicated blackness.

The only trouble with nightgoggles is that they cut down on your peripheral vision; I had to keep my head moving from side to side, always wondering if the next thing to swim into view would be a stooping t'Tant.

I turned to look up at Elweré, spread across half the sky. Elweré was alive in the dark. Through thousands of plexi windows, light pulsed crimson. The rainbow

walls were still rainbows in the dark, but the colors
were now different shades of orange and red, cascad-
ing through all the tones of that part of the spectrum.

Looking at Elweré was like looking at another world.

I forced myself to pay attention to what I was doing.
It didn't take much effort; I knew that I had to be
careful. Though, with a bit of luck, there would be no
t'Tant over the city tonight. After all, the vrasti had
almost all been exterminated in the city, their nests
found and burned; there would be little to hunt.

But there were still some nests at the edge of town,
where the valda fields started.

I scanned the dotted blue sky. Off near the horizon,
three yellow specks circled over a distant valda field. As
I watched, one stooped, skimming below the horizon
for a moment, then climbed back into the sky, wheeling
over its hunting grounds.

I walked on. As I reached the foot of Baker's Row, I
ducked into a doorway, trying to ignore the light and
sounds from inside the barred windows.

That's the nice thing about being a buzh, I guess:
visiting. When they visit each other late in the day, it's
understood that the visitor will spend the night safely
within his host's house, protected by solid doors and
iron bars. When times are good in Middle City, the
night-long parties must be fun.

Even in bad times, it must be nice to spend an evening with a friend.

After walking down Baker's Row, I passed by Joy
Street. There, the sounds were louder than usual, the
music gayer. In the afternoon, Joy Street was frequented
partly by buzhes, but mainly by the lower classes of 'port
employees. At night, it was the turn of pouch-heavy
shipmen and the higher-ranking Commerce Department people; only they could afford the price of an

all-night orgy behind the barred windows of a fancy Joy Street house.

An orange shape passed over me, less than a hundred meters overhead; I dove under a porch, retrieving a concussior from my pack. A concussior isn't a powergun, but it just might serve the purpose, if my timing was right, and if I was *very* lucky. It would have to detonate within a meter or so of the t'Tant's body—a concussior's explosion is mainly light and sound—and that was unlikely. I'd never heard of anyone successfully using a concussior to take on a t'Tant; I'd never heard of anyone trying.

But if I was attacked, the concussiors were my only chance. I shivered as I crouched there, my thumb on the detonator.

Seconds passed, although it felt like hours.

Nothing. Maybe the t'Tant hadn't seen me; its attention could have been elsewhere.

I peered out. Half a kilometer away, the orange t'Tant flapped through the royal-blue sky. It hadn't seen me.

I rolled out from under the porch, brushed myself off, and continued toward Elren's shop.

Generally, when you're burglarizing, the best way to enter a building is from the roof. Not necessarily *through* the roof—although that's often good—but *from* it. It's just a matter of applied hominid psychology; our species is used to attacks from ground level. People don't tend to think of the second or third stories as being as vulnerable.

I'd never burglarized at night before; I'd never been out at night before. During the day, though, there's another advantage to going in through the top: humans tend to be interested in what's at their eye level nd below; looking up is an acquired behavior, not a atural one.

Climbing up to the third story wasn't difficult; I vorked my way around to the back of the building, trapped on my ankle and shin spikes, and then slipped n my climbing gloves.

The gloves were awfully well made; I had cut and titched them myself. Genuine cowhide, shrunk to fit kin-tight, each glove containing three sewed-in, spike-ipped steel bars, curved to accommodate the outer three ingers of each hand. It left me a bit clumsy, but I :ould still manipulate with my thumb and forefinger, while hanging from a sheer face, as long as I could dig he spikes in.

A quick glance at the sky, and I scurried up the side of the building like a spider.

I was breathing hard as I pulled myself up to the roof and stretched out flat on my back, my eyes search-ng the sky, my ears primed for any sound.

There were a few t'Tant off in the distance, but they were too far away to worry about.

Good.

I picked my way through the rubble and pipe scat-tered across the roof. There's always a trapdoor of some sort leading to the roof; it took me only a couple minutes to find it.

At first, it looked good: a heavy steel plate, the hinges heavily shrouded, with a pull-ring in its center.

I pulled, but nothing happened. Not surprising; it was likely deadbolted from the inside.

Oh, well, life isn't supposed to be easy. I'd have to do it the hard way.

I walked to the side of the building away from the street and unstrapped my bag, laying it gently on the roof. I pulled off my gloves and dropped them on the bag. They'd served their purpose.

I took a length of rope and my coilsaw from the bag,
put the saw between my teeth while I tied a bowline in
one end of the rope, then took a quick eye measure of
the distance from the edge of the roof to the corner
window. It was about a meter and a half to the bottom
of the window; I'd want the loop to be just at roof level.

I fed the other end of the line through the lip, and
belayed it to two jutting pipes. Standing in the loop
would be idiotic; I could easily fall over. On the other
hand, hanging upside down wasn't going to be fun, but
I could stand it for the few minutes it would take for
the saw to cut through two or three of the bars on a
window.

After another scan of the sky, I tightened the loop
around my ankles and pushed off the edge of the
building.

I looked inside. The room was empty, save for a few
rolled rugs hanging from the floor. My head started to
pound as I hung there, but I ignored it as I wound the
saw around a bar and then waited, listening. There
hadn't been any lights in the building, or any sounds,
but it was always best to take the extra moment to make
sure.

Nothing. Pulling first on one handle of the coilsaw,
then the other, it took me a scant minute to slice through
the bar. It was low-grade steel. Understandable; it was
intended to keep out t'Tant, not me.

Another minute, and I cut my first slice through the
second bar, then started on the second slice. This was
going to be a bit tricky; there were lights in some of the
other houses, and I didn't want either of the bars to
clang on the ground below.

Working quickly but carefully, I sawed almost all of
the way through the bar, until it dangled by a thin
shred of steel. I gave the other bar the same treatment,
then put the saw back in my mouth as I bent upward

first one bar, then the other, working them back
d forth until they both snapped loose in my hands.
I slipped them inside the window until I felt them
ch floor. Leaving both bars propped against the
ndowsill, I pulled myself back up to the roof, intend-
g to take a few minutes to get my breath back before
ing inside.

Intending to . . . I heard the rush of air from behind,
d threw myself down between two pipes, the t'Tant's
ws missing me by scant centimeters.

It wheeled around the sky, readying itself for the
xt pass.

I didn't wait around to see if it would be luckier this
ne; I snatched up my shoulderbag, grabbed onto the
pe, jumped over the edge of the roof, and swung in
rough the gap into the room.

My shoulderbag bouncing out of my hands, I landed
all fours in the deserted room, then quickly got to
y feet and moved to the side of the window. The gap
tween the leftmost remaining bar and the edge of
e window was half a meter—not enough for the t'Tant
fly through, with its wings extended, but more than
ough for it to drop through with its wings folded, if
got up enough speed and aimed its body correctly,
unting on its levitating ability to make last-moment
inor corrections.

If it could think of that. Which I doubted, but wasn't
ing to bet my life against.

I picked up one of the steel bars. If it tried to get in,
might be able to knock it back outside before those
zor-sharp claws sliced me into thin strips.

Maybe.

Minutes passed. Nothing. That was good; the t'Tant
d given up.

Retrieving and donning my shoulderbag, I walked to

the door and put my ear to it. No sound from the oth
side. Slowly, I opened the door, stepped out, th
closed it behind me.

The hallway was a royal blue, lit only by vague r
traces of starlight peeping under the three doorwa
that led to outside rooms.

The walls, floor, and ceiling were blue outlines, bare
visible. There's only so much that nightgoggles can d
this wasn't nearly enough light to see by. I took n
flash from my pouch, dialed it to low by touch, a
thumbed it on.

Much better. In its crimson light, the hallway leap
into clarity. It was narrow, about forty meters lon
with rooms opening up on both sides. There was
staircase at either end; I moved quietly toward th
nearer.

At a thin scuttling on the stone floor behind me,
spun around, my improvised bludgeon raised.

Nothing. Just bare floor, a wall table set underneat
a painting, and a closed door leading to the roo
beyond.

I shrugged. It had sounded like a vrasti's claws. Not
ing to be worried about, although the presence of vras
marked Elren as a lousy housekeeper.

I smiled. Too bad for her.

Still moving silently, I worked my way down the ha
tiptoed down a wide stairway, and crossed to the do
of the room where Elren and I had done our busines

I turned the doorknob. Actually, I'd expected it to b
locked, but it opened at a touch.

Strange. I walked inside.

Using the bar to probe at the rug in front of me,
worked my way over to the desk. There was no sign c
boobytraps or alarms.

I shrugged. I guess Elren trusted her guards an
locks in the daytime, and the predatory t'Tant at nigh

The desk locks were Earthmade Yales—Model XXVI, Catalog #339837(A) in the Montgomery Sears catalog, in case you're interested—which raised another smile. Those are fine locks, so fine and so popular that Carlos had given me half a year's worth of training on how to pick just that make and model.

I took my lockpicking kit out of the bag and used the thin plastic probe to feel around in the space between drawers, but there wasn't anything. No triggers, no wires, nothing.

Oh well. I brought out my lockpicks and got down to work.

The top drawer took me only a couple of minutes. Inside were a few odd coins, a small wooden box filled with what looked like diamonds but what I was sure were only yags, a scattering of flimsies, a bottle of pills, and the other sorts of valueless detritus you'd expect to see in a desk drawer.

If that's all there was here, why bother locking the drawer?

I'm sure you figured that one out; there was only one answer: the purloined-letter trick, the idiot version—as in both *by* and *for* an idiot.

I pulled the drawer out and placed it on the desktop, measuring it with the calipers from my lockpicking kit. Sure enough, there was a full three-centimeter gap between the bottom of the inside of the drawer and the bottom of the outside.

Finding the catch was tricky; Elren had been very clever. It took a full thirty seconds.

I lifted off the false bottom, and, scattered among rings and gems and stones of all sizes, there it was. Amos van Ingstrand's brooch.

She hadn't broken it up. Which meant either that she was being very clever, biding her time until she could move it offworld, or . . .

. . . or she was hanging on to it, to sell it whole back to van Ingstrand, along with the identity of the man she'd bought it from.

It didn't matter, not anymore; I tucked the brooch into my inner sleeve pouch, dumped the rest of the rings and gems into my shoulderbag—including the yags, on the grounds of *why not?*—and spent half a second debating whether or not to look for other valuables, as long as I was here.

I guess that Carlos One-Hand trained me too well; I reached for my picks.

That greed saved my life. If I'd walked to the door . . .

As I was working on the first side drawer, there was a scrabbling outside the door, and five hand-sized vrasti ran in, concealing themselves—or trying to—in the curtains.

Behind them, the door swung gently open.

And three t'Tant, flying single-file, flapped slowly after them.

Later, it all made sense: the lack of alarms, boobytraps, or human guards; the loose security; the vrasti in the upstairs hall. Elren Mac Cormier was cheap. Instead of shelling out coin for any normal type of protection, she had merely offered the t'Tant access to a building filled with tasty vrasti—plus a possible occasional burglar, as a side dish—in return for being locked in for the night. The only cost would be live-trapping some vrasti—or maybe she raised them in the basement.

A fine deal for the t'Tant, and one that their daylight selves would easily find agreeable. In the morning, both the sunlight streaming in the windows and the bright electric lights in the house would make it safe for her to show them out, quite possibly through the trapdoor in the second-story ceiling.

It all made sense much later, but right then I stood

stock-still for a long moment, dumbfounded, not moving until the nearest of the t'Tant was within inches of my face, its claws outstretched.

I ducked down, under the desk, pulling my shoulderbag with me. One of the t'Tant landed behind the desk and began clawing at the shoulderbag, trying to get at me. Most of the damage was to my bag, but as the t'Tant slashed it to ribbons, spilling the contents over the floor, one of its claws drew a long gouge down my left arm, ripping my tunic.

I kicked at the t'Tant, and felt wingbones crunch as I knocked it away, but that didn't make things any better: a fresh t'Tant took its place.

There was no way out. The t'Tant could easily keep this up until morning, and morning was hours away. I couldn't hold them off for long.

My fingers scrabbled on the ground, looking for some weapon, something, anything that would buy me a few more seconds of life.

They fell on a concussior; I snatched it up. Kicking at the t'Tant, I tried to find another, but the rest of the contents of my bag were too widely scattered. I could see two other concussiors on the floor, but if I tried to reach out and take them, all three t'Tant would be able to get at me.

Blood ran down my arm and onto the concussior. Maybe, just maybe, it would shock them, stun them just long enough for me to get at the other concussiors, and perhaps the bar. One steel bar against three t'Tant wasn't much of a chance, but it was my only chance.

I thumbed the concussior and flicked it out into the room, squeezing myself farther back into the recess, fighting to keep the t'Tant's claws away from my face.

Whomp!

The concussior went off, deafeningly loud, the light

so bright it leaked around the eyeseals of my goggles. They flared into a bright red as their circuits overloaded.

Everything went black; the goggles were dead.

Blindly, I kicked at the t'Tant. It fell away limply. That was strange.

I yanked the goggles off my face.

The three t'Tant spread their wings in the dying light of the concussior, chirruping merrily, ignoring the flames licking at the base of the curtains behind them.

I didn't take the time to think it through. I dived out of the protection of the desk, scooped up my last two concussiors, thumbed and threw one, then ran out of the room, my ears already ringing so loudly I didn't hear the sound of its ignition as it flashed behind me.

It was the light, of course; the bright light of the concussior had awakened the t'Tants' plant brains, which were much more interested in tasty wavelengths than tasty me.

I crept back through the dark night, my eyes on the sky, the brooch heavy in my sleeve. I'd managed to beat Elren Mac Cormier's security system, and while I'd lost my pack, I'd gotten what I came for. I could sell the brooch to Benno. Without it as evidence, Elren wouldn't dare approach van Ingstrand, no matter how angry she was. She would know that old Amos would kill her for first having, then losing it.

Safe. For the first time since I'd been idiot enough to steal the damn thing, and even more of a fool to turn it over to Carlos One-Hand, I was safe.

I felt very clever, all the way home.

The floor of the tunnel was littered with slivers of stone. Someone had triggered one of our boobytraps.

I dialed my flash down to low, until I could barely see in its dim glow. Normally, I wouldn't have worried

bout it. All that meant was that someone had tripped
one of our warning traps; likely, whoever it was had
run off.

But, combined with everything else, it was better to
play it cautiously. I crept forward, listening for any
sound, my one remaining concussior ready in my hand,
just in case.

As I approached the rubble heap that blocked off
our home, I heard a distant moaning from inside.

Slowly, silently, I climbed up the heap and looked
down.

Carlos One-Hand lay on the green everclean rug,
naked and dead, dark pools of his blood already
congealing, blind eyes staring up toward the ceiling.
They'd worked him over thoroughly before killing him,
but what could he had told them? That I was supposed
to be here, but that I'd sneaked out when he went to
sleep?

That wouldn't have earned him even a quick death.

But where was Marie? She was only a child; maybe
they wouldn't have hurt her. I slid down into the room.

She lay curled in the corner. Carlos was dead, but
she was worse. "David," she said, her voice cracking in
pain. "Make it stop hurting. Please."

My stomach rebelling, I pawed through a pile of
booty. There was some valda oil, somewhere around;
that would help. I'd have to get some help, but where?
How could I find help at night—

There was a voice behind me. "Good evening. We've
been waiting for you, David." A large blocky man, his
tunic splattered with blood, sat on top of the rubble
pile, a crossbow leveled at me.

He gestured with the bow. "Over here, please."

I triggered the concussior and threw it at him, diving
for the control box in the corner as I did. The bolt

whizzed past me, tugging at my tunic as it buried itself in the rug.

Whomp!

The light beat at my closed eyes; the noise deafened me, but I reached the box, thumbed it to live, and pushed the button.

There was a louder explosion, beating dust into the air as the tunnel collapsed over the entrance to our home, burying the man, blocking the others outside, at least temporarily.

My head spun as I turned back to Marie. There was nothing I could do for her, as she lay there, her eyes pleading with me, her mouth working. Our back door was a rough, narrow tunnel; I could barely squeeze through it myself. Pulling her behind me just wasn't possible.

And she would need help soon, or she would be dead. They hadn't been gentle with her.

Please, her lips said, *make it stop hurting, David.*

I did.

God forgive me, I did.

I lowered myself to the floor of the shaft outside the back door, then dropped the rope. I wouldn't need it, ever again. I wouldn't be back there, ever again.

But what could I do now? I was wanted by Amos van Ingstrand—though he couldn't have wanted me any more than I wanted him dead—and now even Lower City wouldn't be safe for me. Carlos and Marie had certainly described me for his men; my makeup kit was back inside.

And I wasn't going back inside. Not ever.

I had to do something. I couldn't just wait for them to hunt me down. I had to get away. If I could somehow make my way to the 'port and buy passage off Oroga, I'd be safe.

I had to. But where would I get the money? I couldn't
work the markets, not now.

The answer had to be in the warrens. Others lived
here; most of them would leave during the day, trust-
ing to their own boobytraps or lockboxes to protect
their valuables. Not that there would be many valuables.

But that didn't matter. I'd go for quantity, not quality.

After working my way for some distance through the
underground maze, I sat back against the rough-hewn
wall and thumbed my flash off. I'd have to wait until it
was daylight outside and the rest of the warren dwellers had left. That would take hours.

But I had the time. There wasn't anyone waiting for
me.

Please make it stop hurting, David, please. . . .

Not anymore.

I heard that voice all through the long night.

FOURTH INTERLUDE:

Eschteef and the Burglar

Eschteef woke suddenly from a sound sleep, coming completely awake.

This waking was not normal; Eschteef was too alert.

Schrift do not sleep through the whole night. They awaken halfway through their sleeping period for the thyvst. The root of the word is *athyv*—"foolishness"; the time is usually one of slow activity, and temporarily lowered intelligence. The middle of the night was a time for the sorting of low-value gems, or the cleaning of the burrow—any task that required effort, but not great thought or creativity.

So, why am I awake? Trouble for another member of the schtann could awaken it, of course, but it was almost alone in its head; the others still slept.

Strange. Eschteef had not wakened in the night since it was a youngling.

Eschteef eyed the chrono mounted over the door to its sleeping niche. It lacked more than an hour until its usual time of thyvst.

So, why do I awaken? At a quiet whisper of sound from the outer room, it rose from the blanket-lined depression in the floor, keeping itself in a half-crouch.

There was something in the outer room, something that felt strange. Eschteef opened its mind. No, this was not one of the schtann, but there was something. . . .

Eschteef peered through the curtains, into the outer

room. Holding a hand flash, a young human stood over its work table, brushing scraps of silver and gold into a bag.

Strange. . . . Eschteef quelled its first instinct, to attack and eat the thief. This was the same boy who had reacted to its chrostith in the marketplace the day that the human van Ingstrand's brooch had been stolen. Eschteef had felt something in its head that day, something that might almost have been cherat.

It had reported that to Hrotisft, expecting an explanation. Hrotisft had given it only abuse.

‹Nonsense,› Hrotisft had said, with a hiss partly of irritation, partly of amusement. Theoretically, it was possible to feel cherat with an alien; yes, there had been alien members of other schtanns, and even a few such members of the metal-and-jewel-workers schtann, but no *human* was worthy of membership in the metal-and-jewel-workers schtann. ‹The poor creatures,› Hrotisft had said. ‹And poor Eschteef! I am the one who should be losing its faculties, not you.› It had hissed again.

Eschteef hadn't liked that hiss. Alerting the rest of the schtann would only expose it to more abuse, more laughter.

It would deal with this human itself.

One way or another.

CHAPTER SIX:

"It May Be of the Schtann. . . ."

The second-to-last place that I burglarized was relatively easy.

Back when the silver mine was operating, it must have been a storage room for valuable tools, or perhaps explosives: the carved-out room was secured by a solid steel door set into the stone, secured with a combination lock.

I had to be careful. It was several hours since I had last heard people returning home down the corridors—now it was night outside, and the room was likely occupied. Conceivably, once I solved the lock and started to open the door, the hinges would squeak, alerting whoever was inside to my presence.

The door was large and heavy, probably of offworld import. I had high hopes for its hinges. The combination lock, on the other hand, looked and felt local. As I turned it, I could feel that the lubricant inside had long since worn away. I could practically hear the tumblers click; it was no challenge at all.

The combination ended with a solid thunk as all the secondaries fell into place. I turned my flash off, pushed on the latch, and slowly pulled at the door.

It swung open silently on what were, no doubt, imbedded-silicone hinges. Bless the Earthies—when they

et their little minds to it, they can make things that last
orever.

I stood silently in the dark, listening to the deep
nores of the sleeper inside. A sound sleeper, I hoped.
walked inside, dialing my flash to low by touch.

Over in the corner of the room, someone slept under
pile of blankets, food rinds and winebottles scattered
round him.

There was nothing much worth taking—a few pouches
f beef, a bottle of wine. Whoever lived here was almost as poor as I was; the most valuable thing he
wned was the combination to that door. Leaving the
vine, I scooped the food pouches into my bag and left,
losing the door behind me, and worked my way deeper
nto the warrens.

I paused in front of a massive wooden door, shaking
off my exhaustion. I was deep inside the warrens now,
nd quickly running out of options. I didn't have any-
hing near the price of a ticket, and I still hadn't found
nything that could serve as a disguise, something to
give me a decent chance of going out into the city,
working my way to Benno the Exchanger's place, then
booking passage offworld.

Not to mention that I didn't have anything to trade
to Benno for enough tweecies for a ticket.

But this was interesting; this door blocked the tunnel.
Not a side room—either there was a cul-de-sac beyond,
or, just conceivably, a large section of tunnel, with
something in it worth protecting. Possibly something
worth stealing.

I shone my flash around the door frame and smiled.
Good—there was a pressure latch at the top of the
door. When someone opened the door, the latch would
spring open. And something would happen. Most likely
a deadfall would drop. Anyone who set up an explosive

boobytrap would require some way of turning it of and I couldn't find anything that indicated a keyhole

That, combined with the height of the door, su; gested that the resident of whatever was beyond was schrift. With its great strength, a schrift would find deadfall that could crush me flat as a flimsy no problem the creature could just catch it as it fell, then lift it bac into place.

I snapped my blade into my hand and wedged it int the doorframe, just under the catch, working it we into the wood. That would keep the catch closed, an the deadfall from falling.

I turned off my flash, and slowly, carefully, swun the door open. It moved silently.

I stepped inside, feeling my way with my toes, lister ing intently for any sound.

Nothing. Which was good. But I couldn't stumbl around in the dark; I'd have to risk a light for moment.

I dialed my flash to low and took a quick look around It was a rough-hewn, three-meter-high room, the wall and ceiling above the tunnel's normal two-meter heigh smooth, as though it had been chiseled out by someon taking more care than would be normal for a minin; tunnel. Against the right-hand wall, an elaborate woode workbench stood, tools lined neatly in carved recesses three large piles of metal scraps. The left-hand wal held cabinets and a cookstove. The back wall wa; covered by a beaded curtain.

This was it. I'd found a schrift jeweler's home.

I doused my light. Perhaps I was being overcautious but quite possibly the schrift was sleeping beyond tha' beaded curtain.

No problem; I had the location of the table marked in my mind. Moving with exquisite slowness, I worked my way across the stone floor, reached out over the table, and scooped the scraps of metal into my bag.

I crouched there, hefting my bag and debating whether or not to risk a light again, feeling like a hunted animal.

Which wasn't far from the truth.

If it was really silver scrap that I'd taken from the table, if the schrift had enough confidence in its dead-fall to leave silver—or even gold—lying around, if there had been a valuable jewel or two in the pile—if, if, if.

But I had to know. If I had enough in the bag, I could take my haul to Benno, trade it for enough tweecies to buy a ticket off the planet.

For where? I really didn't know. It really didn't matter. Anywhere there wasn't a bounty on my skin would do. That would be enough for now. Later, I would find somewhere where there was a lot to steal. I had much stealing ahead of me, over the next few years; it would cost a lot to hire enough mercenaries to be sure of killing Amos van Ingstrand.

Slowly. Very slowly. Worse than he'd done to Marie.

I shook my head. That wasn't for now; no point in even thinking about it. For now, I had to see if I had enough to get off Oroga. If I didn't have enough, maybe I could hunt around, find the schrift's main cache. It had to have one—possibly in the room, possibly outside. This couldn't be all the metal and gems that a schrift jeweler would have.

To hell with it. I set the bag on the floor and pulled my flash out of my pocket, covering the glowplate with my fingers, trying to keep them from shaking.

I thumbed it on and spread my first two fingers, careful to keep the narrow beam of light from flickering around the room. If the schrift was sleeping beyond the curtain, I didn't want to wake it. If it wasn't, but was heading back toward its burrow, I wanted to be sure that I saw it before it saw me. Anyone—well, almost anyone—would turn me in for the reward that van Ingstrand was offering. He wanted me badly; a hundred thousand pesos is a lot of money.

I spread the mouth of the bag and shined the light in. There were dozens of oddly shaped scraps of some whitish metal that could have been silver, or iridium, or platinum—I'd be able to tell better when I got it in the sunlight—and there was gold. Buttery, yellow, wonderful gold.

Enough to take to Benno. He wouldn't turn me in. An exchanger can't betray a customer; it's bad for business.

I forced myself to calm down. Just because what I had was valuable didn't mean that it was enough.

Hmm . . . the gold was worth maybe five thousand pesos; the silver, perhaps twice as much, altogether. The brooch in my sleeve pocket was worth a hell of a lot more, but Benno wouldn't pay me more than a couple of thousand for it, under the circumstances. Figure he'd give me ten thousand pesos for the lot.

I ran a rapid series of calculations. The official peso/tweecie exchange rate was a little more than forty to one. A Gate ticket to anywhere was just over two hundred tweecies; assuming standard conversion rates, this was more than enough. But it wouldn't be safe to take the money to the preserve for conversion; van Ingstrand's people would be watching.

That left Benno again. And he was known for discretion, not generosity. I'd be lucky to get one hundred fifty from him.

No, I'd have to look for more. And if not here, then elsewhere. But it wasn't likely I'd run into another bonanza like this one; best to strip the schrift's lair of everything valuable that I could carry.

As I raised my light to look around the room, it bounced out of my trembling hands. Too much fear in the past couple of days; too little food.

The flash rolled noisily across the stone floor, coming to rest in a rut.

The light sprayed across the wall next to the door. In the middle of the circle of light, like a butterfly pinned to a plate, was a wooden shelf, set in a roughly hewn niche.

And on the shelf was the silver pitcher, the one that I'd seen in the marketplace.

It was still beautiful. Despite everything, I stood still for a moment, drinking it in.

There was a voice behind me. "No, little one, it is as I told you. It is my chrostith. It is not for sale. Or for thieving."

Carlos One-Hand had once explained that the main difference between lifting and burglary is that in the first case, if you're caught, there may be some benefit in pretending to be innocent; in the second, the only chance is to run.

I didn't look behind as I leaped toward the door. Once out, I could lose whoever it was in the tunnels. All I had to do was get past the—

The world exploded into fire, and heat, and then black.

Carlos used to train both of us to come awake quickly by sneaking up on either of us while we were sleeping and resting the point of a knife against his chosen victim's throat. If we grabbed his hand before he touched us with the knife, we'd get a reward: not having to sleep with him for five days, sometimes longer. Little Marie was good at it; eventually, he gave up on giving her the chance.

I was horrible. I can never seem to wake suddenly;

always, it's been a slow swim back up to the real world. Sometimes I'm tempted to drown in my dreams; they're always nicer.

This time was as bad as it's ever been. I was dreaming about my mother again, I think. All I remember was soft hands and gentle voices. Then again, that's all I've ever remembered about her.

And then there were other voices, in a strange language. Not too strange; Carlos had made me learn some Schrift. At one point, it was the height of style for Elweries to address each other in Schrift. I guess he figured that when the same fad rolled around again, I'd be ready for Elweré.

‹—so why do you keep it, Eschteef? The human, Amos van Ingstrand, does offer whoever turns it in a hundred thousand of Elweré pesos, two thousand frusst of silver, or a hundred of gold.›

The other voice whistled nasally: a schrift chuckle. ‹I keep it because it may be of the schtann.›

‹That is foolishness. We have discussed this before.›

‹No, Hrotisft, we have *not* discussed this before. I have reported a strange event to you, and you have mocked me. There was a moment just now, and another one, days ago. I felt something. Perhaps cherat, perhaps not. It will cost little to find out. A bit of time, a few bowls of food.›

‹I still say that this is—›

‹And there is another reason to keep the little human, at least for a while. The reward may go still higher; it may be possible to negotiate through the Exchanger for both child and the brooch that it had in its sleeve; we may be able to get more silver and gold.›

The brooch! I pressed my left arm against the stone. My sleeve was empty.

‹Eschteef, do not be greedy.›

Another nasal whistle. ‹Hrotisft, my teacher, first

ou accuse me of foolishness; now, of greed. If you
ccuse me falsely, your age is getting the better of you;
truly, it does not speak well for you, that you spon-
ored such a greedy fool into the schtann.›

This time, the other whistled back. ‹My age? You
ay that—very well; do it your way.›

I'd waited long enough, trying to get my bearings
ack. It was tough; a clout on the head hard enough to
nock you out leaves you aching, nauseous, and disori-
nted at best; it can easily leave you brain-damaged, or
ead.

The stone floor was hard under my cheek. All it
ould take would be a quick leap to my feet, then a
ash for the door. I'd pull my blade from the deadfall's
atch as I passed, blocking the way behind me.

I opened one eye. All I could see was rock; the
chrift had left me facing the wall.

I sprang to my feet, forcing them to stay underneath
ne. As I did, I heard metal scraping on stone.

Three steps toward the door, and my right leg was
erked out from underneath me. I slammed hard against
he ground, half blind with pain, my shin aching horribly.
reached down to rub it.

No wonder I couldn't run; my right ankle was clamped
n a metal cuff, the cuff connected to a chain, the chain
olted to the wall.

The larger of the two schrift leaned over me as I lay
n the floor, painfully pulling air into my lungs. I'd
nown that the schrift was a huge creature, but it
eemed even larger close up.

The head was a mass of gray skin, with two deeply
et eyes that seemed to burn from an internal fire.
There was no hair on its head; only two widely spaced
aasal slits on its face, earholes to the side. Nothing of
nterest except a cavernous mouth, with sharply pointed

teeth. I wasn't sure if I believed that schrift actually a
human flesh; I wasn't sure if I cared.

Maybe that would be better than being turned ov
to van Ingstrand, having him flay the skin—

Tears welled up as I remembered Marie, begging m
to make it stop hurting, please, David, make it sto
hurting, please, please . . .

‹Do you hurt?› it asked in Schrift, then shook m
and hissed the question in Basic when I didn't answe
"Do you hurt?"

Blunt fingers reached down and felt at my ankl
easily brushing my hands out of the way as I tried t
protect myself. "Don't worry, little human. Not yet
The hot, dry fingers were strong, but the schrift touche
my scrapes gently. "A bruise or two, but you are no
badly damaged. I may have some valda oil—"

‹And what use have you for valda oil, Eschteef.
The other schrift hissed. ‹Have you changed into
human without my knowledge?›

‹No, Hrotisft, it was the thief who tried to ste:
from my stall.› This one—Eschteef, that was its name—
rose, and rummaged through a bin near where I lay
‹It had a small vial on it; I have not bothered to tak
the time to sell it, yet. I think it is—ah.›

The schrift dripped a few drops of the cool oil ont
my shin, then rubbed it in, the pain receding as thoug
I had had never been hurt. The scrape was still there
and the bruises soon would be, but not the pain. Tha
was the value of properly treated valda oil: the mole
cules wrapped themselves around free nerve ending
only; it eased pain, without doing any damage to nerve
or other tissues.

Eschteef raised its head. ‹Go now, Hrotisft. Yo
seem to frighten the human child.›

‹Easily solved.› Hrotisft snapped its jaws. ‹Eat it
or sell it to Amos van Ingstrand—›

‹Hrotisft . . . the matter is closed. For the time being, at least.›

‹Very well. I will return in a few days. Or sooner, if needed.›

‹Of course.›

Hrotisft lifted the stone deadfall with one six-fingered hand, slipped the bar into place to secure it then closed the door behind itself.

Eschteef lifted me to a sitting position and crouched down in front of me, in an awkward-looking squat. Schrift always looked funny to me. Their forearms and lower legs are disproportionately large for the limbs, and the limbs themselves are too thick. Of all the sapient races, they're the most disturbing to look at; they're shaped too much like humans.

‹Do you understand me?› it asked.

"I don't know what you're saying," I answered in Basic. No point in letting the schrift know that I understood its language.

Eschteef stood and moved swiftly but gracefully to the niche near the door. That's another disturbing thing about the schrift: the way they go from stillness to quick movement, and then back to motionlessness, as though they have no inertia.

Carefully, gently, it lifted the pitcher from the niche, cradling it in its fingertips as it brought the pitcher back to me. "This is my chrostith, my . . . master-work-so-far. I have had two other chrostiths, two other creations that deserved to be called the best that I, Eschteef of the metal-and-jewel-worker's schtann, could accomplish. And this is better than the second, as the second was better than the first. And someday, there may be a fourth, if my hands are steady enough, my mind clever enough, my . . . heart worthy." Its eyes didn't move from my face as it spoke. "Almost always, a member of my schtann creates one chrostith; frequently, two; rarely, three; four or five, almost never."

I could understand that. How could any creature be able to top something as beautiful as this?

Eschteef held the pitcher half a meter away from me, as though it wanted it close enough for me to appreciate, but far enough away that it could easily prevent me from touching it, if I tried to.

But I wouldn't have. It was beautiful. Not beautiful as in "I can make a lot of money with this." Just beautiful. Perfect.

Even with all the pain in my head, all the tired aching that made the tendons in my shoulders burn like hot wires, I sat back, and let the wonder of it wash over me.

Just as had happened in the marketplace, I felt something. A little twitch in my head, like an electric warmth in my brain. And then it was gone.

‹Yes,› the schrift said, bringing the pitcher closer, ‹perhaps the human child belongs in the schtann. It's not unknown. There have been human members of other schtanns, and other alien members of our schtann. There was a brace of poncharaire many years ago, as I recall. Perhaps the human child is simply retarded—›

"I am *not* retarded. Carlos One-Hand said that I was the best lifter he had ever seen, except for himself and . . ."

and Marie. I wept.

Eschteef rose and took the pitcher back to its niche, setting it down as though it were a priceless piece of glass.

‹Since it is apparent that you speak my language, we shall cease the pretense, keh?›

With a nasal whistle, Eschteef drew the curtains back from a cupboard and brought out an earthenware pitcher and two stone mugs, each half the size of my head.

After filling the cups, it set the earthenware pitcher on the table that I'd taken the silver and gold from before, and brought both cups back to where I still sat, chained to the wall.

It squatted in front of me. ‹You see, little one, I have a problem. If you are not destined to be part of my schtann—and I am by no means certain that you are . . .› It took a scrap of cloth from its pouch and wiped my eyes and nose. ‹Humans.› A hoarse tick issued from its throat. ‹More different kinds of bodily fluids than I can see a reason for. They drip at every orifice, I do swear—if you are not of my schtann, then I should—and I will—turn you over to Amos van Ingstrand, and claim the reward.› It gestured toward my now empty sleeve pocket. ‹And sell the brooch back to it, as well.›

It handed me a cup; I drank deeply. Mannafruit juice; it washed the blood and dust from my throat.

Eschteef tilted its head back, until its mouth pointed toward the low ceiling, and poured the liquid in.

‹More? Good. But if you are of the schtann, if you can become of the schtann, then I must aid you and train you. Of course.›

I shook my head. It didn't make any sense. "I don't understand. A schtann is like a family to you, right?"

‹That is almost correct. And you wonder how you and I could be family, keh? But Schtann is more than family, little human. It is . . .›

I didn't understand the next words. I knew some Schrift, but I wasn't all that proficient in the language.

The schrift switched back to Basic. "Very well. The schtann is the group of beings with which one is . . . in communion. A part of the whole, losing nothing by the commonness, gaining much. There are many schtanns among the schrift: the childgrowers, those who bring younglings through their final transformation into adulthood; the producers-of-meat-and-drink, those who cause food animals and fruit trees to flourish and grow; the builders, who dig in the ground and lay one block on another . . . and my schtann, the metal-and-jewel-workers, we who create beauty from gold and diamond.

"But there is always one thing in common: cherat. A . . . meeting of the minds—"

"Telepathy." I shrugged. Except for the common latent sensitivity to psi, telepathy is a rare gift among humans; maybe one in ten million has it. I'd never met a telepath; the Thousand Worlds sweeps in all nonlatent human telepaths to be trained by, and part of, the Contact Service. "I'm not a telepath."

"No. Not simply telepathy. Cherat is more subtle; a sharing of emotion, not only of gross thought. Members of my schtann share the beauty of our work together; we care with one another."

Like that tickle in my mind when I'd looked at the pitcher.

I shook my head. "It can't be."

‹We shall see. . . . Tell me, what were you doing here? And with this?› Eschteef held up the brooch.

The truth couldn't hurt. "I stole it from Elren Mac Cormier." But why should I tell it all of the truth? "She must have bought it from whoever stole it from Amos van Ingstrand."

The schrift hissed. "A poor lie. What did you plan to do with it?"

"I was going to sell it to Benno the Exchanger. Figured to buy a ticket off Oroga."

"Ah. Benno the Exchanger. I have dealt with it. A shrewd man; it does not give very good value. Why did you choose it?"

"He's the father of a friend of mine, a girl on Joy Street. I know he wouldn't turn me in."

"True. But not for that reason. It is discreet, is Benno."

The blunt fingers stroked my brow. "But why are you here? Risking robbing a schrift? If not to avoid Amos van Ingstrand, then why?"

I wept. Marie . . . Carlos . . .

"These others, you hurt for them."

"*No.* I don't. I don't care about anyone, about anything." You can't care about people, not if caring means that you see them lying on the floor, their flesh flayed from their bones, the remains of a face turning upward toward you, saying make it stop hurting, David, please make it stop hurting, David, please. . . .

I'll kill you, Amos van Ingstrand. I swear that I'll kill you.

"Be silent, little one. Rest. You begin training tomorrow. If you are of my schtann, you'll learn to care."

‹This is a circle of sheet silver—›

"I know what silver is."

Eschteef set the disk down on the table in front of me, laid the rubber hammer gently between it and the concave stone bowl form, then grasped me by the hair with one hand and gave me a firm slap with the other. It gave out an almost human sigh, then picked up the hammer and the silver.

This had been going on, off and on, ever since it woke me, fed me, brought over a stone bucket for me to use as a chamber pot, then unbolted my chain from the wall and brought it and me over to the work table.

I hadn't tried to escape. Yet. Eschteef was always there, and it was stronger than me. But it'd have to sleep sometime, and even if I didn't have the strength of a schrift, I was sure that with a few hours to work in, I could use its tools to free the chain from the wall, if not the cuff from my ankle.

But where would I go? Gina would probably hide me for a while, but that wouldn't solve anything. I'd need money or silver, and plenty of it.

Best to wait for a while. See if I could spot where it cached the brooch, and the rest of its silver, gems, and gold. Just a matter of time.

‹This is a circle of sheet silver, and this is a hammer, keh?›

"*Yes*. This is a circle of silver, and this is a hammer." *And that is a knife over there, and if you move just a little bit, I'll see what color your liver is, you filthy, stinking lizard.*

It must have seen me look at the knife, although I swear I only glanced at it. ‹No, little one, it would not be wise, even if you could cut through this thick hide of mine. The schtann would come.› It picked up the knife and set it down farther down the table, well out of my reach. ‹Best not to tempt you.›

It set the bowl form and the silver disk in front of me again, then placed the hammer in my right hand, wrapping my fingers around the smooth handle. ‹The grip must be sufficiently tight for control, but not too tight, or the hand will tire; tired hands make mistakes.› It moved to my side, squatting next to me, then picked up a duplicate of the hammer I held, and took the silver disk in hand.

‹Now. We incline the circle of silver *so*›—it fitted the edge of the disk into the bowl—‹and strike it with the hammer *thus*.› It struck the disk firmly, halfway between the center and the edge.

‹You try.› It gestured at my disk. ‹Try to strike it as I did, your blow overlapping mine.›

I gripped the disk, resting the heel of my hand on the table; no point in putting in any more effort than necessary. I gave the disk a solid whack.

"*Oww!*"

Eschteef caught my hand, my aching thumb just inches from my mouth. ‹Never put your hand in your mouth. This time, it would be harmless, but you will be handling many substances. Most pickling solutions are poisonous to me. Do humans drink sstraszta?›

"*Sstraszta*? I don't know that word."

Eschteef paused for a moment. "Acids." ‹Do humans drink such?›

I wasn't sure whether or not it was making fun of me, but I didn't want to get slapped again. "No."

‹Perhaps that is something else you would not care to learn how to do. Now, try again.›

It adjusted my fingers around the now-bent silver disk, keeping my thumb well away from the striking area. ‹Do not worry; everyone hits itself now and again. Even Hrotisft, who taught me, has a scarred thumb. And it is as great a member of the schtann as ever there was.›

Eschteef had started rambling on again. Just like Carlos, Eschteef was always talking. But with Carlos, I'd learned to use that: while he was telling me how great a thief he was, he'd usually leave me alone. Maybe . . .

I spoke in Schrift. ‹What do you mean, that the schtann would come?›

Eschteef took the hammer and disk from my hand, then set them in front of itself. ‹So, your finger—thumb, keh?—hurts enough that you would rather talk than work.

‹Cherat is the transfer of emotion, keh? Among the emotions are fear›—it used the Schrift word *kstak*, of course—‹and ryvathkstak, the fear-of-oncoming-death. Were I to feel ryvathkstak, others of the schtann would hear me, would come to my aid. Cherat was how I called Hrotisft when I heard you in this outer room. I had intended to deal with you myself, but there was that flash of what might have been cherat. So I called Hrotisft. I could have called the whole schtann, but . . .›

"You didn't figure to need more than one other to help you chain a human. Maybe you should have called for more," I said, eyeing the knife.

‹It was not necessary. You have rested enough; try again.›

I took up the hammer and hit the disk again, not denting it as much as Eschteef had.

‹Better. But strike more firmly. Your purpose is to mold the metal, not simply to attract its attention.›

As I kept banging at the disk, it kept talking. ‹If you can become part of the schtann, you will always feel cherat with the others, appreciate the work of their hands, feel their love for the work of yours. When you can do work worth loving. Not this.›

Eschteef took the battered disk from me and began to shape it with its own hammer. ‹If this is the best you can do, I will have to sell you and the brooch to Amos van Ingstrand. This is not the work of even a youngling member of the schtann. Observe.›

In a few moments, it had shaped the battered disk into a round-bottomed bowl, covered with the scaling of the indentations of the hammer strikes. Working with another form, it bent the lip inward, curling it over.

‹You see? So now we have a bowl. We may inscribe its sides, or flatten the bottom as a base, or make a separate base and weld it on. I think we will both flatten the bottom and then inscribe it—but first, we shall place it in the oven, to smooth the marks from its side. We will have done this together, little one.›

Eschteef's hand was oddly clumsy as it patted me on the head. ‹And when you can do this all by yourself, drinking in the beauty of the work and the working, sharing that with others . . . you will be part of your schtann. You will not be so alone anymore.›

I nodded. Not that I meant it. Everyone is always alone. If someone feeds you, it's because he wants you to steal for him, or he wants to bugger you. If someone smiles up at you, trusts you, looks up to you, you come home to find her dead. Or worse.

Eschteef lit the finishing oven and set a pot on top of it. ‹You may use my spoon and eating prong today. But you must make your own bowl—if you wish to eat.› It pointed a claw at the stack of silver disks. ‹Begin.›

CHAPTER SEVEN:

"This Is What Eschteef Teaches You?"

I started learning the next morning. There was a lot to learn; it sank in like water into sand. . . .

‹Seaming is the process of joining two or more edges to form a cylinder, loop, or cone. The key to any seamed work is the joint, which must be prepared as follows. . . .

‹When raising a vessel from a silver or copper circle, the first issue is to decide on the size of the initial blank, keh? You must begin with a perfect physical or mental model of the finished vessel. The general rule is this: take the height of the finished vessel, then add to it the average diameter of the finished vessel. That will give you the diameter of the blank you will require. This rule is not useful for vessels which will have a broad, flat base and a narrow neck—you will require a larger blank. . . .

‹Burns are a hazard which are sometimes unavoidable when working close to hot metal. Most burns can be prevented by foresight; all can be minimized by proper safety procedures. Being a human, you will be tempted to overestimate the value of valda oil. Do not: it eliminates pain, not damage. Nerve tissue will not grow back, and some loss of dexterity is likely. . . .

‹The objective in diamond-cutting is to maximize the number of visible facets, while minimizing the amount of wasted diamond. This brings out the brightness and life of the gem. Cutting may also be used as an opportunity to remove a localized flaw. . . .

‹Stainless steel is one of the most difficult alloys to work with. Damages to the surface are difficult to repair to the point where the flaw will no longer be visible; they are impossible to repair to the point where the flaw will no longer exist. . . .

‹Steamcasting is not an effective technique for bronze. The metals react together and create escaping hydrogen gas; the cast becomes pitted at least, craterous more likely. . . .

‹Enameling silver is an alloy of unusual purity; its high melting point will allow you to heat enamels applied to it until they are able to cure. Do not use enameling silver for normal applications. . . .

‹Gold is the most forgiving metal; mistakes are easy to correct. The purer the alloy, the more this is so. . . .

‹Wires have three basic uses. First, they can be functional—as in a bezel, for instance. Second, they can be decorative—as ornamentation welded on to a ring. Third, they can be both functional and decorative. This is the highest use. . . .

‹You must never clamp metal with metal. Use wooden or plastic blocks in the vise. For very delicate work that requires clamping, carving or casting a negative is suggested. . . .

‹Small holes in a piece are best polished by string. You insert one end of the string—like so—and work it back and forth. . . .

‹The interior of a piece should be finished before the exterior. There are no exceptions to this rule. . . .

‹There are innumerable techniques available for texturing of surfaces. They include carving, engraving, polishing, flame texturing, etching, chasing, stamping, planishing, piercing, sawing, shotting . . .›

I never left Eschteef's burrow in the next year. I slept when I was sleepy, ate when hungry, and spent the rest of the time learning to bend, raise, anneal, fold, engrave, and planish metal; to cut, polish, and mount gems; to work wire into useful and decorative shapes.

I never stopped thinking of Carlos and Marie, of killing Amos van Ingstrand, or of escape.

But escape was impossible; Eschteef never slept while I was awake. When it had to go out—to bring its work to the stall in the marketplace, to buy food or supplies— there was always another schrift dropping by, just as it was about to leave.

I didn't mind that much. It was nice to see another person. Even Hrotisft, with its constant, barely veiled threats.

‹This is what Eschteef teaches you? I know that humans are clumsy, but this is ridiculous. Better it should sell you to Amos van Ingstrand. Better that, than disgracing the schtann with this work.›

‹This is *good*,› I snarled, "you stupid old lizard."

I held the carved silver box inches from its eyes. ‹What is wrong with you, old one? Are you losing your sight, as well as your deftness?› Hrotisft was old, even for a schrift; it could barely keep a riffler steady in its hands.

I had a right to be angry. I'd spent the better part of twenty waking periods just making the hidden hinges perfect, so that the jewelbox would whisper open or closed at a touch, and much more time than that carving the designs on all twelve faces, inside and out.

‹I lose nothing! I am of the schtann. You are outschtann—and nothing but a thief.› It pushed me over to the table. ‹Look, outschtann!› It slammed the box down on the table with one hand, grabbed the back of my neck with the other, almost grinding the tip of my nose into the top of the box.

‹*Look!* You have carved the gem mountings too shallowly, you lazy human; were any gems set, they would have bounced out just now. You must add raised bezels, not think yourself finished.

‹*See!* Can you not see that you have carved lines across the face of the box just to take up space, not to create beauty? Have you eyes, or have you not?

‹*Observe!*› It picked me up by the neck and threw me halfway across the room, ignoring the sounds from the tunnel.

The door opened, and Eschteef stood behind Hrotisft, lowering its packages to the floor. ‹And if I say that the human can be of the schtann?›

‹Then you lie. Or mislead yourself.› With that, Hrotisft left.

Eschteef helped me to my feet. ‹Do not be angry with it, David. It is old, and frustrated.›

‹Frustrated?› I slammed my fist against the wall. "What right does it have to be *frustrated*? It isn't the one chained here like an animal. It isn't the one who has to perform or be turned over to van Ingstrand. It isn't—"

‹Keh. Hrotisft is not the one. Hrotisft is not many things, anymore. Mostly, it is not young. Metals and gems used to obey its wishes, as though of their own volition; now, Hrotisft can barely control its own hands.

‹And it resents you, little human. You are not of the schtann, yet your clever fingers have learned quickly.

‹But Hrotisft feels no cherat with you. Your work just lies there. It has value, yes, but you are greedy; you hoard your appreciation, you do not share what you have done, what you are.

‹Hrotisft is old, and tired, and lives only for the

schtann, David. It should be bringing younglings into the schtann, educating them, but that is not possible on this world. There are few better places for a metal-and-jewel-worker to practice its trade than outside of Elweré, but there are no breeding ponds here.›

I shrugged. ‹So build some. The schtann has money.›

‹And who would raise the younglings? There are no childgrowers here; should we import that schtann? Should they trust us not to take advantage? Should we trust them? No. Schrift will always be alien to this world; we live here only for a time, to produce beauty and earn credit. And then we go home, back to Schriftalt.›

‹So why doesn't Hrotisft go home?›

Eschteef stood silently for a long moment. ‹I don't know. It won't say anything more than that it is needed here, for now. And that gives me hope, David, but also worry.›

I didn't understand, but I didn't say anything.

Eschteef went on, as though to itself. ‹Hrotisft has always had a better feel for the way of things than I. But if you are to be of the schtann, I can teach you. Unless . . .› Eschteef shook itself all over. ‹But enough of that. You must learn to feel more deeply, David, to become part of your work, and let your work become part of the whole. You only do; you feel nothing, and are poorer for it.›

"That's not true, and I wouldn't care if it was!"

‹Then why do *tears* stream down your face? Sit, David. You must get back to work. Hrotisft was wrong about your box; it has . . . possibilities. Now, what sort of gems had you intended to mount, and where? Those mountings will not do, though. Let us try . . .›

I looked at the box. Not bad at all. Matter of fact, it was damn good. And it felt good, too, like lifting a pouch off a sober, sharp-eyed inspector, the kind who always keeps his hand on his money. . . .

The lines curving all over its outside faces made a pleasing contrast, as though denying that the box was really rectangular.

It was nice, except for the firestone in the middle of the cover. A fine stone, yes, but inappropriate. Its fiery reds clashed with the gentler hues of the onyx and emeralds.

Eschteef stood across the table from me. It's hard to tell what a schrift is thinking when the creature is silent; their facial muscles aren't used for cues, and the body language was too subtle even for me, someone who can tell whether or not a victim is conscious of his dangling purse by the set of the shoulders, position of the head.

‹It is almost right, David. Except for that firestone. It throws off the color balance. The purpose of decorating with gems is not merely to add colors and shapes, but to add the *right* colors and shapes, each in its proper place.›

‹I know.› I bit my lip. "Dammit. It needs something powerful right there, but not that colorful. It just looks . . . gaudy, that's all."

‹What would you like to substitute?›

‹An aqua, I suppose. Not as riveting as it should be, but it would be in accord with the color balance.› I raised an eyebrow.

‹You do not need additional colors. Consider something relatively color-neutral.›

Not a bad idea. "Maybe a yag?"

‹Why settle for yttrium aluminum garnet? It is only a false diamond. You might as well use a piece of cut glass. If the piece requires a diamond, then use a diamond.›

"*Great* idea." I caught myself. Eschteef didn't understand sarcasm. ‹No, it is not a good idea. Where would I get a diamond that size?›

‹From midair, I suspect.› Eschteef's hand moved suddenly. The diamond caught the light of the oil lamp and shattered it, almost hanging in the air in front of my eyes.

Thief's reflexes took over; I caught it before it even came near the table. "Where did . . . ? The brooch."

‹Yes.›

‹Then you are not—›

‹I broke it up the day that I told Hrotisft that you might become part of the schtann, David. The day I caught you thieving.›

My hands shook as I gentled the firestone out of its bezel, replaced it with the diamond, then crimped it into place. Not quite perfect: I'd want to cut a deeper well, use a smaller bezel.

‹It is fine as it is, David.› Eschteef just sat there, its appreciation of my work washing over me.

We were both silent for a few minutes, just sitting there, appreciating. As though I was part of the schtann, almost.

Which I wasn't; I couldn't feel the others. Eschteef was in my mind with me, but only Eschteef.

‹Eschteef?›

‹Be silent, little one.› It rose and walked over to the tool bench. Without a word, it took up a chisel and hammer and proceeded to remove my cuff's rivet.

The cuff fell to the floor with a clang; I rubbed at my ankle, eyeing the doorway.

But I didn't run; I couldn't move. Eschteef walked to the niche in the wall, drew the curtain, and took down its chrostith, and turned about to face me.

‹This is my chrostith, David,› it said. ‹Only one of

my schtann may touch it, only one who will share its appreciation with me.›

It held the pitcher on the palms of two outstretched arms.

‹You will hold it, David,› it said.

"But . . ." what could I say? *But I'm crippled, retarded. I'm not of the schtann, Eschteef. I can't be part of anything. That wasn't cherat I felt; I could only feel your appreciation, your love of the work of my hands. I couldn't feel the rest of the schtann with me. Not the way you do, every time you touch a bar of silver, feel an onyx's smoothness.*

‹The rest will come, David. In time. We will have to bury your past, but we will do it. Take it.›

‹But, Eschteef—›

‹You are of my schtann, David. You will hold my chrostith.›

I held the pitcher in my arms.

And wept.

CHAPTER EIGHT:

"You Will Return. . . ."

The six schrift formed a half-circle, six pairs of eyes focusing like a lens on the foot of the table.

Guess who got to be at the focus of the lens?

‹Try again, David,› Eschteef said. ‹Let yourself feel; let us into yourself.›

"I don't remember volunteering to be the subject of a schtann inquisition," I said.

Hrotisft sniffed. ‹I do not recall asking whether or not you cared to volunteer. You are here for us to determine, on behalf of the entire schtann, whether or not you can become a member of the schtann. Your wishes in the matter are not relevant.›

‹Please try again,› Eschteef repeated. ‹I know you can be part of us.›

I looked at Eschteef's chrostith again. It was still beautiful, of course, and I felt that.

In the back of my mind, there was a vague reflection of Eschteef; of it feeling a tingle of acknowledgment of my appreciation, but that was all.

‹I feel no cherat,› Sthtasfth said, its voice flat, expressionless. ‹If the human can become part of the schtann, this is no evidence.› Sthtasfth was the largest of the schrift, a gray monster half again Eschteef's size. Eschteef had shown me some of its work; curi-

112

ously enough, Sthtasfth produced the most finely detailed work of any of the hundred or so members of the schtann within Lower City. Sthtasfth was a precisionist—grafthisth, in Schrift. In order to fully appreciate the pendant that Eschteef had shown me, I'd had to use a magnifying glass.

Rhathsfoosf held itself perfectly still.

‹Neither do I.›

Eschteef pounded the table. ‹You can feel cherat with me, can you not?›

Rhathsfoosf turned to it. ‹Of course.›

‹Then observe.›

Eschteef took my box down from a wall niche and set it in the middle of the table.

It was a strange feeling. Eschteef's appreciation washed over me like a warm benediction. And, for just a moment, I could feel distant reflections of the others joining in its feelings.

But only for a moment. The feeling passed.

I was alone inside my head, as always.

Hrotisft took the box in its hands. ‹The work is good, but lifeless. The child has potential.›

Staring at me, Rhathsfoosf spoke up. ‹But there is no cherat between the child and us. Perhaps there is none at all. Eschteef could be deluding itself, only wishing to feel cherat, for reasons known to all of us: it has yet to bring any younglings into the schtann; the human child is perhaps but a substitute.›

‹I *do* feel cherat with the human,› Eschteef said. ‹And if you doubt me, then—›

Hrotisft toyed with a piece of scrap silver. ‹Eschteef, this is not the way. We must accept that you feel what you say, and you must accept that we feel no cherat with the human child.›

‹So? What do we do? You wish to turn it over to

Amos van Ingstrand? I will not permit it; the human is part of the schtann.›

‹We will not turn in the child,› Hrotisft said. ‹That is not an issue. For now.›

‹Then—›

‹But it is not established that the child can be part of the schtann.› Hrotisft sat silently for a long moment. ‹David?›

"It's about time you stop treating me like I'm just an object. You—"

‹Silence. You are here to be examined, not to vent your anger. Tell me about›—it worked its mouth awkwardly, fumbling for the Basic word—"fhamily."

I shrugged. "Family? What do you want to know?"

‹Why is this concept important to you? Eschteef says that you are distressed that you do not know who provided your genes.›

Distressed. I guess I would have been offended if Hrotisft's voice had held even a trace of condescension. But it didn't; only curiosity. "Wouldn't it bother you not to know who your parents are?"

‹No. It does not. It distresses none of us. Our species lays both kinds of eggs in breeding ponds; none of us know who provides such.› It hissed. ‹It is possible that Hrotisft could be a *mother* of Eschteef—›

‹No,› Eschteef interrupted, with a light hiss, ‹you are what the humans call *male*, keh?›

‹Yes, but—›

‹The *male* is the *father*, not the *mother*. The *mother* provides the motionless part of the egg.›

‹I do not understand,› Rhathsfoosf said, gesturing apology for the interruption. ‹Humans have a different word for the providers of each part of the egg? What is the importance?›

‹They breed while in the same place; it is necessary to pair a provider of the moving part of the egg with a provider of the motionless part. That one contains its own hatching grounds in its belly.›

Air whistled through Sthtasfth's teeth. ‹It keeps a pond in the belly? How terribly unsanitary. Humans are disgusting.›

Hrotisft gestured for silence. ‹The point is that what is normal for us may not be normal for this human. The relationship between the two providers of genes and the youngling seems to be central to humans.›

‹Disgusting,› Sthtasfth repeated.

‹Perhaps. But it is the way of their species. This *family* seems to serve some of the same functions of schtann: protecting the young, as the childgrowers do; teaching of skills; and the giving a sense of belonging, as all schtanns do. But this human does not know who its providers were. Eschteef says that seems to distress it.›

Rhathsfoosf made a pushing-away gesture, as though to dismiss the subject. ‹The human child is fortunate not to know in whose belly its growing pond lies. Sthtasfth is right; these habits are disgusting. What has this to do with whether the human can become part of the schtann?›

‹I think that I see.› Eschteef held up a hand for silence. ‹If there is a bond between child and *parents*, that may be what is holding David back. It cannot sever the bond, because it cannot see it.›

‹Precisely,› Hrotisft hissed. ‹It may be that what needs to be done is for the human child to discover who its providers were, so that it can cut that connection.›

That didn't make any sense to me. Not at all. What did one have to do with the other? Even if I knew who my father was, it wouldn't make me part of the schtann. I couldn't be part of anything; I couldn't allow myself to feel part of anything.

But it did to the rest; the other schrift murmured their agreement.

Hrotisft went on: ‹That is as far as I can grind the thought. We must find out who David's *parents* are, but I do not know how.›

Threstast spoke up for the first time. ‹We must think and polish the thought. If this relationship is important to humans, they must keep records, keh?›

‹Reasonable.›

‹Then, we must get access to these records. And if such exist . . .›

‹Yes.› Hrotisft hissed. ‹They must be in Elweré.›

‹Very well.› Threstast gestured an acknowledgment. ‹But how do we find them?›

‹I have a plan,› Hrotisft said. It stood and walked to the storage bin in the corner of the room, pulling out bars of gold and silver and small sacks of gems. ‹We have much work to do.›

I didn't argue. Not then.

I'd never known who my parents were, and I wanted to, every bit as much as I wanted to slip a knife in between Amos van Ingstrand's ribs.

The doubts came later.

"You don't understand, Eschteef," I said, as we walked toward the outsiders' entrance to Elweré. "If my father finds me, he'll have me *killed*. The Elweries don't like to have bastards running around; they consider it shameful."

‹Enough of your complaining, David. There are, at present, more than seven million members of the schtann in the Thousand Worlds. And the *Elwereans*—please stop calling them Elweries—know that we do not take the killing of one of our own lightly. The problem is getting you to the security station without alerting the watchmen. That is all.›

The sun hung low in the sky; merchants were folding up shop and preparing to go home for the night. Assuming that we could get into the outsiders' areas at all, we wouldn't be able to spend much time doing whatever the hell it was that Eschteef intended that we do there before we would have to get back. Even a chrift can't expect to take on t'Tant.

‹Were I you, little David, I would be more concerned about Amos van Ingstrand's people's spotting you.›

I wasn't terribly worried about that, not at the moment: in a baker's smock, with my hair lightened a shade or two and my skin darkened more than that, it was unlikely that anyone who didn't know me well would recognize me.

Besides, there's one advantage to walking with a chrift: people tend to keep their eyes on the hulking creature, not on its shorter companion. It occurred to me that this could be used as a nice lifting routine. Maybe I could get Eschteef to growl threateningly, while I worked the crowd. That would be fun.

I'd need to get together some money. I was a thief, not an assassin.

But there was no urgency about dealing with Amos; that could wait. For years, if necessary. I'd want to be in on it, and I wouldn't be able to face doing that until I could close my eyes and go to sleep without hearing *Please, David, make it stop hurting. . . .*

‹It is very strange,› Eschteef said, a note of disbelief in its voice. ‹All this preoccupation with sources of genetic material. Ahh, let us stop here.›

We paused in front of a poster.

REWARD   REWARD   REWARD
The Lower City Protective Society offers 100,000 pesos for information leading to the apprehension of a thief known as DAVID (last name, if any unknown). . . .

*   *   *

... it began, and went on into a description of me
and my offenses: my lifting of a valuable piece of jew
elry belonging to someone unnamed; my burglarizing
and torching of Elren Mac Cormier's shop ...

My offenses. This from Amos van Ingstrand.... My
hands started to ball themselves into fists, but years of
training took over, and I acted like a young baker's
apprentice would, one who had seen the poster several
dozen times, but still dreamed of claiming the reward:
I read the poster up and down, studied the sketch
carefully, then walked on with Eschteef.

"Eschteef?"

‹Yes, David?›

"How sure are you that we can do this?"

‹It should be relatively simple,› it started.

I snorted. I'd heard that before.

‹No, David. It should be. You know how the Elwereans identify themselves before reentering the city;
they have no fear of lowers trying to enter.›

We were almost past the last row of stalls in the
Lower City markets. I turned to Eschteef. "But how do
we get close enough to the Elweries' entrance?"

Eschteef hissed. ‹Trust your own skills, David.›
Eschteef hefted the bag that it carried. ‹And ours.›

The narrow road twisting up toward Elweré was almost deserted, occupied only by a few merchants, bringing sly grins and the remains of their unsold merchandise
back down toward Lower City. Selling to the Elweries is
always rewarding.

We got a few curious glances, but not many; nobody
wanted to stop and inquire what a schrift and a human
were doing going up toward Elweré this late.

‹Here,› Eschteef said, handing me the bag. ‹Behind
that bush.›

I ducked behind the bush and stripped down to my

are skin, then opened the bag. First I took out the small plastic containing the damp washcloths, and quickly rubbed both makeup and dirt from my body.

And then I dressed: the one-piece undergarment, followed quickly by a new segren tunic and a black teak dominoe that fitted my face perfectly. I slipped on and belted the white silk trousers and hung a silver-mesh pouch from the belt, then pulled on the calf-high leather boots.

Then the accessories. First, a finely worked ring for each finger. They fit perfectly; I worked my fingers rapidly, enjoying the flashing of jewels in the sunlight.

‹Enough vanity. Finish dressing.›

Then, a sheathed silver smallsword, with a well-worn bone hilt. Inside Elweré, it was a dueling sword, used with a slip-on stopguard for minor duels, as-is for second- or third-blood duels. But outside of Elweré, it was just for show; an Elwerie's—Elwerean's—real defenses were in the harness.

I took my harness out of the bag, slipped the many-lensed band over my head, settled the leather yoke on my shoulders, then examined myself in my hand mirror.

Not bad at all: I looked just like an Elwerean.

Granted, it was all an illusion, but it was a good one.

The lenses on the headband didn't contain cameras, and while they were wired to a small steel box at the back of the harness, the wires and the rotating nozzles on the harness itself were just an effect. Under Hrotisft's supervision, the others had been able to create an imitation of an Elwerie's apparel, but actually making the workings of twin powerguns and the circuitry necessary to control such were beyond them.

‹I will meet you up there, David. It is best that we not arrive together.›

"I understand." *And the last part of the disguise. . . .* The mental part of it was never more crucial than it was now, and never more difficult. Of course, I'd seen a few Elweries in Lower City; yes, I'd studied their customs and practices so that I could learn how to imitate them.

But that wasn't enough; I'd have to live it.

I stood up straight, my shoulders back, my neck held stiffly upright, then examined myself in the mirror.

That was right, but it wasn't enough. Even with the dominoe obscuring my features, I still looked scared, like a lower pretending to be an Elwerean.

I had to get the inner disguise just right; I forced myself to feel confident, to know that I was just . . . Leif Ortega, that was a good Elwerean name. I was Leif Ortega, returning home after a long afternoon spent between fresh sheets in a Joy Street house, that following my morning's exercise of shopping in the Lower City markets.

But it still didn't look right. Ahh, if I was coming home from the markets, where were my purchases? Drawing the smallsword, I cut a ragged piece of cloth out of the shoulderbag, wrapped it around a stone, then stuffed it in my pouch.

Better. And if I was back from an afternoon at Joy Street, I should be a bit more tired; I let my shoulders sag a trifle, then rubbed my fingertips over some imaginary scratches on my ribs.

The mirror bore me out: I was ready. I walked up toward the entrance, and through the vaulting archway.

I stood on the broad floor, forcing myself to breathe a sigh of relief, as though pleased to be home after a hard day of shopping and sex.

The room was large and high-ceilinged, the walls decorated with gold-and-pearl-inlaid friezes, the ceiling minutely carved. The floor was thousands of square meters of white marble, no doubt imported from Earth itself.

Next to the far wall, three Elweries had finished making their purchases from the six schrift jewelers. Tucking their bundles into their pouches, they walked over to the security station. One by one, they unbuckled their harnesses and dropped them in a bin as they walked past the first guard, then past the guard sitting at the security panel, and lined up in front of the niche in the far wall.

One at a time, each Elwerie pressed a thumb and an eye into the appropriate recess.

And, as each was scanned, the light above the niche flashed green. The guard pressed a button on his panel; a door slid down over the niche, only to slide up in a moment, revealing it to be now empty.

The six schrift jewelers were finishing their packing. I swaggered over to the table, pretending to examine the racks of rings and pendants.

"Khind ssir," Eschteef hissed. "Whould you honor uss by examining our wares?"

‹Your accent is horrible,› I said. ‹Who taught you Basic, Hrotisft?› I smiled.

‹Don't be more of a fool than is absolutely necessary, young idiot. The guard may know some Schrift,› Hrotisft said, its words belying the gentle tone of its voice.

‹Walk away now,› Eschteef said.

I moved slowly toward the guard station, Eschteef and Hrotisft following, brandishing a double handful of pendants, as though haranguing me to buy their wares.

As I started to unbuckle my harness, the guard stood, loosening the safety strap from his holstered powergun.

I forced myself to return his overly broad smile.

"Are these schrift bothering you, young senhor?" he asked.

"Not at all. Were they," I said with a sneer, "I could handle them myself, no?"

"Yessir." His face whitened a touch as I let my hand fall to the hilt of my smallsword. If I drew it, it was a no-win proposition for him. His best bet would be to hope that I only wanted to frighten or wound him. If an Elwerie wanted him dead, he would be dead.

"We'll let it pass, just this once." Ignoring the schrift behind me, I walked into the niche and pressed my eye against the lens, slipping my thumb into the notch.

A light flashed behind the lens; coolness washed my thumb, followed by a light sting.

The lights around the niche flashed red.

I spun around. Eschteef had pulled one guard away from the panel; Hrotisft, with a strength belying its advanced years, was holding the other over its head with one hand, the other hand clamped tightly over the guard's holster. In a moment, Hrotisft was joined by two of the other schrift, while the remaining two helped Eschteef to spread-eagle the panel guard against the wall.

Eschteef's hand was at his throat; the guard could barely gasp.

"We will be gentle with you, human, provided you help us."

The guard's eyes bulged as he gasped for breath. "I . . . can't let you in. The panel only allows me to let someone in if the green light flashes."

I stood in front of him. "We don't want you to let me in. That machine says I'm not registered as an Elwerie, correct?"

He didn't answer. Eschteef tightened its fingers around the guard's throat for a moment, then loosened its grip to allow the guard to gasp for breath.

"Y-yes. It says you're an impostor."

"What you will do," Eschteef said, "is use the machine to analyze who the human is. You will find out who its father is from the blood type—that is possible, no?"

The guard tried to shake his head. "No. It can't be done."

"Try," I said. "Try real hard. You have access to all the ident records, no?"

"Yes. I have to—"

"Better run some sort of comparison. Or else."

The guard nodded.

Eschteef and Sthtasfth frog-marched the guard over to his chair and seated him ungently.

Sthtasfth produced a thin wire and wound it loosely around the guard's neck. "If there is trouble," it said, "I can pull this through your neck in less time than it will take for your heart to beat for the last time. Are we agreed that there will be no alarms?"

The guard nodded, and began working the panel, his hands moving slowly. "You'd better hope that Central doesn't get curious as to why—"

"No," I said, "*you* had better hope."

"Fine, fine. Just let me do it, okay?" He glanced at the readout and tapped twitching fingers against the keyboard. "Blood type double Ay—that's good; both parents are Ays, Ar Aitch pos, Dee En at seven part per mil, Oh Eff neg, whites type . . ."

My heart pounded. Maybe I'd never know who my mother was, but at least this would tell me about the father that abandoned me, kept a reward out for my life. Was it my fault that I was a bastard? I hadn't chosen to be one. What kind of person could hold that against me?

In a moment, I'd know.

Granted, the schtann's notion that this would solve

anything was ridiculous, but you couldn't blame them
the notion of it being normal for someone to know
who his parents are was so strange to them that it was
understandable they'd attribute what they thought of
as my disability to my being, well, normal for a schrift.

The panel flashed red; the guard's eyes grew wide
"No—*it wasn't me*. The entry's flagged." He paled as his
head turned toward me. "You're *David Curdova*."

Sirens began wailing; the door to the outside slammed
down with a deafening thump.

Hrotisft's hand covered Sthtasfth's. ‹Do not kill the
human. I sense that there is no harm for the child
here.›

The man's brow wrinkled. "You don't know who he
is?"

Hidden panels in the walls swung open. Twenty security men, half of them struggling into their coveralls,
stormed into the room, power rifles drawn.

Their apparent leader, a grizzled buzh with sleep-red
eyes, held his gun steady on Hrotisft. "Don't make a
move toward the senhor, or we'll cut you all down."
The rest of the security team covered the others. He
jerked his chin at me. "Senhor. Please step away from
the schrift. Everything is under control."

I didn't move.

"Please." He turned to the man at his side. "Mick, get
over between the senhor and the schrift."

‹David?› Eschteef reached out a hand. ‹Don't be
afraid. We will protect you.›

‹There is no need for that,› Hrotisft said. ‹As I
sensed.›

One of the buzhes moved; I jumped between Eschteef
and the gun.

"*No*." The leader kicked the gun away. "My apologies,
senhor. These are friends of yours?"

I stood dumbfounded. *Senhor?* The most I'd ever gotten off of a buzh was a pitying look and a full purse.

I managed to stammer out a yes.

"Fine. But we're not going to take any chances. You, the schrift holding the wire. Drop it, and move away from the senhor and the guard."

‹Do as they say,› Hrotisft said.

Sthtasfth complied.

The guards moved in and formed a circle around me. "You sure these are friends, senhor? We'll blast them for you, if you'd like."

It didn't make sense. They'd decided that I really was an Elwerie? Might as well play along with it. "No. There is no need."

"Fine. Mick, do you think we should get them out of here, or hold them for the old senhor?"

"Let them go; he'll be too busy with the young one. And dealing out credit slips right and left." Mick chuckled. "Love this blind dumb luck, eh?"

"Shut up. You schrift—get out." He gestured toward the steel door to the outside, then spoke into his shirt microphone. "Area secured; we have him."

"Understood," the distant voice sounded. "Senhor Curdova is on his way. Art, this had better be the right goods; I had to wake him."

"Check the ident board, idiot."

"Hmmm . . . congratulations, Art. You're a rich man."

The schrift stood still.

"Move." The leader snarled at them.

Eschteef moved in front of him. "I will not let you kill the child."

"Kill him?" The leader was almost as dumbfounded as I was. "His father would have me flayed if I so much as *bruised* him. He's Miguel Curdova's son, you know."

Hrotisft moved to Eschteef's side. ‹It is as I suspected. The child is not *illegitimate.*›

‹Then why all *this?*› Eschteef's voice was weak.

‹Would you have believed me? You thought the child was of our schtann. No. It is of Elweré.›

‹No. I felt the cherat—›

‹Then ask it. Ask it would it rather stay here, with its parents, or come with you.›

‹David?›

Behind me, the door to the niche swung open, and a middle-aged Elwerie walked out, doffing his dominoe, throwing it aside.

It was like looking in a distorting mirror, one that reflected back my face, aging it. His cheekbones, his nose, the sharpness of his chin ... they were my cheekbones, my nose, my *face*, only a generation older.

"Father?"

He smiled through the tears, then set a grim expression on his face and drew himself up straight. "Kelly."

"Senhor." The leader of the guards brought himself to attention.

"Are these schrift the ones who stole my son, kept him from me?"

"Doesn't read that way, senhor. Looks to me like they're trying to return him. But the boy seems scared about something, like we were going to hurt him." He raised a palm. "I swear we didn't threaten him, senhor, but he didn't seem eager to come with us."

‹He will not. The child is part of my—›

‹Silence,› the Elwerie hissed back. He turned to me. "Have they hurt you?"

"No ... but I—"

"Later." He smiled. "We'll talk about it later." He turned to Hrotisft and spoke in heavily accented Schrift. ‹You have my gratitude for the return of ...› He struggled for the right word; there isn't a Schrift word for "son." ‹... the youngling.› He jerked his chin at he guard. "Kelly, give each schrift ten kilos of gold, nd send them all on their way."

"Yes, senhor."

"David, come this way." His arm around my shoulder, e pulled me toward the niche.

I wish I could say that I was torn, that I struggled vhether to go back with the schtann or into Elweré vith my father—my father!—but I didn't. I turned my back on Eschteef and walked toward the door into Elweré.

‹David,› Eschteef called, so low I could barely hear him, ‹you are part of my schtann. You will return.›

CHAPTER NINE:

"You Are Home Now. . . ."

I should have known. I really should have. I knew that Carlos One-Hand was a liar—and a thief, a swindler, a burglar, a pederast—it shouldn't have surprised me that he had lied about this, about me. But it did. And it hurt.

All those lies about how I was a bastard, about how my father wanted me dead. And the threats to turn me in, and the faked posters advertising for my return, dead . . .

I should have known. After all, having a lower bastard was shameful; my father wouldn't have advertised the fact for all to see. If I'd just thought it through more, or talked about it more, if I'd just mentioned the posters to Gina, she'd have figured it out.

I should have known. But I hadn't figured it out. Way down deep, I had trusted Carlos, and he'd betrayed me.

It hurt.

I kept the pain masked as I sat back in my chair, an always-warm mug of tea in my hand. Father wouldn't have understood. I can't really blame him; I'm still not sure that I do.

The room was like nothing I'd ever seen. It was easily ten meters square, the floor covered with an ankle-deep blood-red carpet. Delicate crystal glowglobes bobbed near the ceiling, handmade tapestries covered the walls. I ran an appraising eye over the latter; they were either old Persians or Kazakis; the cheapest was worth more than I'd ever stolen in a year.

And this was just my visiting room; it wasn't even the largest of the six rooms in my suite. At the moment, there were only two armchairs in the room, one for me, one for my father, each of us with a delivery box at his elbow. A nice touch, the delivery box; it would supply anything measuring smaller than about ten centimeters on a side within seconds. When Father had taken a break from our conversation to leave the room, I'd asked for and received three kilos of gold, a sackful of gems, and a small sausage, all of which I'd concealed in my tunic.

No, I didn't think I'd have to cut and run. But it had felt so wrong to be around all this wealth without concealing some.

Miguel Curdova drained the last of his tea, set the mug gently on the table, and smiled. "It's been a long night. Would you like to get some sleep now, or would you rather talk a bit longer?" He hid a yawn behind his hand.

"Just a bit," I said. It had been a long night, though; how do you compress more than fifty years into just a few hours?

I hadn't really tried; mainly I'd listened. *Why didn't you pay the ransom?* I'd asked.

It was a matter of honor, he'd said. *An Elwerean can't be pushed around by savages. It isn't proper. Living as you have, I don't expect you'll understand that, not yet. But you will.*

"Tomorrow, can I see where Mother is buried?"

He frowned at that. "Not quite yet. —Another mug of tea, please." Within seconds, the top of the delivery box swung open, and the steaming cup rose into his open hand. "I don't think it would be a good idea for you to leave Elweré for a while. Not," he said, sipping at his tea, "that I'm worried about your safety, but you've been living among the animals too long. Best that you stay inside until you've had time to adjust."

I didn't press the matter; I had a hunch that Father wouldn't be flexible. Technically, I was a minor, and would be until my sixtieth birthday; for a minor, coming and going from the city was a privilege, not a right.

There were compensations. Minors weren't necessarily subject to the Code Duello.

He brightened. "Besides, you'll have quite a bit to do, between adjusting to life in Elweré and becoming acquainted with all your kin. If we didn't have the door set to privacy, likely your suite would be too crowded for a gentleman to sit in comfort." For a moment, his face clouded over. "Are you *sure* that this Carlos One-Hand is dead?"

I nodded.

"Well, I think I'll have that part of the tunnel excavated, in any case. I'll see that that lower girl is buried properly, with dignity. Pity One-Hand died so easily, but it's best to make sure."

Died so easily. . . . I'd been suppressing it, but that phrase triggered the memory.

David, make it stop hurting, please. . . .

"David!" His lined face was centimeters from mine. "Are you ill?"

I shook my head, trying to clear it. "I want Amos van Ingstrand *dead*."

He turned to my delivery box. "A sleeping potion, please."

"For whom, senhor?" the mechanical voice asked.

"For my son, idiot!" His voice softened. "We'll speak about that in the morning. Not tonight." The delivery box hissed; he brought out a vial and pressed it into my hands. "Drink this; it will help you to sleep. When you have broken your fast in the morning, and are ready to receive visitors, tell a delivery box; I'll join you as soon as I can. For now, good night."

As I rose to my feet, he leaned over awkwardly and hugged me. "It will all be fine. You are home now."

I stood there as the door whisked shut behind him, then walked back to the chair and sat down, the vial still in my hand.

The liquid was thick and green. It sloshed slowly as I fondled the vial.

"This is supposed to feel good," I murmured, wondering why it didn't. I let the vial drop to the floor.

"A mannafruit, please."

"Size, senhor?"

"The largest you've got."

"Yes, senhor. Ten seconds."

The fruit was half the size of my head. I was sure that it was fresh and pulpy inside, but I didn't peel it. I just sat there, holding it, until I fell asleep in the chair.

I awoke the next morning, with its shredded remains in my hands and a bad taste in my mouth, not rested at all.

FIFTH INTERLUDE:

Miguel Ruiz de Curdova and Amos van Ingstrand

Miguel Ruiz de Curdova sat back in his chair, toying with his coffee and an overly large chocolate torte. While he had no affair today, his morning calisthenics had been more vigorous than was usual; he rewarded himself lavishly for both his good fortune and his effort.

The torte's filling was smooth, dark, and rich; the crust light, flaky, and vaguely crispy. Curdova loved pastries, but only rarely permitted himself the luxury of eating them. Not merely because he didn't have the time to work off the extra calories—too much pleasure led to softness.

He sipped his coffee, then set the cup down hard on the saucer, ignoring the way the liquid slopped over the edge and onto the formerly immaculate tablecloth.

The boy didn't fit in, and that was that.

But he should have fitted in; David was his son. The boy should have taken to life in Elweré like a t'Tant taking to the air. David should . . .

Should. That was the operative word. *Should* didn't make it so.

This couldn't go on forever. Eventually, David would reach his majority, and become subject to the Code Duello. The boy's social clumsiness wasn't yet compensated for by a facility with a sword. Eventually David would end up fighting all the duels that Curdova had been intercepting.

And that would quickly lead to a serious wounding. At best. Unless his swordsmanship became better, much better.

Well, there was the germ of an idea: ignore the social graces for the time being, or at least deemphasize David's education in them. Bring in a good fencing master from offworld, and have him train the lad vigorously for a few years.

By the time David reached his majority, he would have to have either social graces or fencing skills, or he would end up dead. It would almost have been better to leave him in Lower City than that.

Blood of my blood and flesh of my flesh—why are you such a disappointment?

No, it was wrong to blame the boy. Curdova had read about other feral children, raised among animals. Thank goodness that the lowers at least had language; otherwise, David wouldn't have even been able to talk.

The fencing-master idea held some promise, though. Train the boy well, let his sword become an almost living extension of his body, then let the sheep worry about offending *him*.

And none of these local bourgeois fencing masters, either, more concerned with style and scoring of touches in a first- or second-blood affair than the realities of death duels. Make the boy a lion; let him be so good, so skilled, that everyone would fear that challenging David Curdova meant a casual decision for a fight to the death.

He raised his phone. "Get me Amos van Ingstrand."

"Yes, senhor."

In a few minutes, Amos van Ingstrand was on the phone, his voice trembling only a little. The fat sadist was worried about Curdova's holding a grudge for the way he had treated David's kidnapper and the little girl. Curdova's only regret was that One-Hand had died easily, and as for the girl . . . who cared about how the animals treated each other?

"What may I have the honor to do for you, senhor?" Van Ingstrand sounded more scared than usual.

Idiot. Having van Ingstrand killed—even speaking harshly to him—would be a tacit acknowledgment of David's former status. And that would result in much laughter in Elweré.

"Where would you go to hire a swordmaster? I want the best."

"The best fencing masters that there are work for Elweré, senhor. I really couldn't say who is best. But I could find out for you, if you'd like," he added quickly.

"No. I don't want somebody who is good at teaching a pupil how to put a scratch on an opponent's arm. I'm looking for a teacher for my son; I need someone with a bit more experience in rough-and-tumble. An Alsatian, perhaps?"

"With all due respect—"

"Keep it short, van Ingstrand. I'm busy."

"Then I'd advise against an Alsatian, senhor. Not if you're really after someone to teach rough-and-tumble fighting. I thought you wanted somebody who could help with Elwerean duels. Perhaps to teach your noble son." There was a trace of choking in van Ingstrand's voice; apparently he still held a grudge against David. Or he was afraid of Curdova's retribution.

Miguel Curdova didn't correct van Ingstrand's misapprehension. Why bother? The fat man's professional opinion was another matter. Van Ingstrand understood violence; Curdova wanted to tap that knowledge. "Why?"

"I once hired one to train some of my men, senhor. It didn't work out; their training is too formalistic. By the time an Alsace-trained swordsman is finished saluting his opponent, the opponent has usually had ample time to book passage offplanet." Van Ingstrand added a light chuckle to punctuate the weak joke. "For serious fighting, better a clod with a truncheon than an Alsace-trained swordsman."

"Your suggestion, then, is . . .?"

"If you're serious about getting somebody good in less . . . formal combat, I'd suggest you send for some-one from Earth. Perhaps La France, or Nippon . . . or, if you don't want a Terran, send off to Metzada, perhaps."

That had a nice ring to it. Get a topnotch Metzadan Master Private, one experienced in combat on low-tech worlds. Have him teach the boy.

He disconnected without the formality of a goodbye.

That just might work. Only a few years left until David reached his majority; let him reach it as an un-couth lion, instead of a socially skilled sheep.

He punched for his secretary.

CHAPTER TEN:

"I Have to Get Out of Here. . . ."

You know what the trouble with rich people is? They don't have enough to do, so they end up with not enough time to do it in. Honest.

Let me take you through a day in Elweré. A kind of a special day, actually. . . .

Morning. Well, there really wasn't a morning in Elweré, not for us Elwereans.

For most of us, that is. Those on the Cortes Generale, like my father and my aunt Therese, rose with the sun, if not sooner. While all of the work and most of the decisions were handled by machines, lowers, or buzhes, there were some things that we had to do for ourselves. Or, actually, that the Cortes Generale had to do for us.

Deciding on the quantity and destination of processed valda oil was the big one, of course, and that was an ongoing process. Valda is handy stuff, granted, and indispensable in surgeries anywhere there are humans—did you know that one out of ten thousand surgical patients used to die in surgery, *just from the anesthetic?* —but Orogan valda oil is only *almost* indispensable. A couple of centuries ago, some bright boy on Earth developed a recombinant strain of *E. coli* that produced minuscule amounts of valda oil.

The bright boy's name was Ernest Castuongway; he

developed the strain in his own labs, fully expecting to end up with the Nobel, the Clairmont, and a hefty bank account. Castuongway got the first two, and sank the money he had received with both prizes into manufacturing the artificial stuff, but he died broke.

Seems that the bacterium is a real bitch to breed; it doesn't like to reproduce, but it sure does like to die. Still, the Thousand Worlds could manufacture its own valda oil; the trouble is that it would cost just over ninety-three tweecies per liter.

So, much of the Cortes' time is given to setting the price of valda, keeping it at just over one hundred fifteen tweecies per liter FOB Oroga.

I know. It's awfully simple math: 115 > 93.

True. Which means that the Thousand Worlds should get valda oil more cheaply by making it than by buying it, particularly when you add in the transportation costs.

But *should* is different from *is*. Every once in a while, another bright boy on one of the Thousand Worlds planets talks about setting up another manufactory, at which point the Cortes Generale nods its collective head and talks out of the side of its collective mouth about how the price can't be lowered. At which point the bright boy *does* set up his manufactory, and the price of Orogan valda drops to about eighty tweecies— delivered—until he goes broke.

That used to happen all the time. It doesn't anymore. One of the jobs of the Cortes Generale is to keep orders low enough so that nobody tries to stockpile long enough to drive our price permanently down. That's what my father does for a living.

Neat work, eh?

But I was telling you about *my* day.

Morning. Well, morning began with a light breakfast in my rooms, either followed or preceded by a lengthy shower. And then a half hour of exercise, closely monitored by my suite's computer. (There is no central computer. Were there, the real power in Elweré would be exercised by the people who operated it, not by the residents. Instead, there were literally hundreds of thousands of dedicated computers, all manufactured and programmed offworld, bought after competitive bids. When one malfunctioned, we turned it off and waited until a buzh mechanic came to replace it. Simple blackbox stuff; we could have done it ourselves, if it wasn't beneath our station.)

Then, another shower, closely followed by another breakfast.

After that, it was almost noon, and time for school. At first, Father had me in a group class, but I didn't fit in with the damn Elwerie—with my younger coresidents. It wasn't just that I was too far behind in every subject—we could have lived with that—I didn't have the social interactions down. What finally ended that was my habit of touching my face when I'm thinking. I knew that was uncouth, but I couldn't help it. Carlos always used to scratch at his cheek when he was thinking, and I must have picked up the habit.

So, I went to school in my suite, usually running lessons off the screen, occasionally visited by one of the three buzhes who had the high honor, distinct privilege, and well-paying job of instructing Senhor David Curdova on the fine points of mathematics, literature, deportment, fencing, dancing, history, languages (my Schrift was a lot better than Sylvia Kodaly's, my language teacher. She spoke Schrift with an audible lisp, which I didn't think was possible), and, of course, economics. Whenever possible, I'd rush through the lessons, so that I could spend some time alone in what was supposed to be my bedroom, but which I'd converted mainly into a workshop.

After school was luncheon, usually eaten in his rooms

with my father, my aunt Therese, my cousin Emilita, or another of my relatives, all of whom would pointedly ignore my lack of social graces.

And then I was free.

Or, almost.

"Father? Can we talk about it now?"

He dipped his already-clean fingers in the blue china fingerbowl, then dried them on his napkin. "No, David. The matter is closed."

My cousin Emilita pretended not to hear as she nibbled at her sweetcake, tossing her head to throw back her shoulder-length light-brown hair. She was awfully attractive; then again, I'd always had a preference for dark skin and high cheekbones, Gina being an exception.

Emilita wore a short dress made of what looked like strands of silver beads that sometimes clung together, sometimes parted. While many Elwerie girls run to fat, she kept herself slender, and her body always on at least partial display. It must have taken constant exercise for her to stay in shape; while she always ate slowly, she ate like there was no tomorrow.

Aunt Therese raised her eyes toward the ceiling for a moment, then sighed. "Kill van Ingstrand for the boy, Miguel. Why not? Does the sight of blood suddenly bother you these days?" While Aunt Therese was only a couple of decades older than my father, she looked much older. Sort of like a fat, aged, three-days-dead corpse.

Her tongue tended toward the sharp. Strongly. I liked her, and the feeling was mutual. She had loved my mother, and the affection seemed to have been transferred to me.

He scowled at her. "Therese, leave it be. I've supported van Ingstrand when others wanted him out. It would be dishonorable to change my stance, merely because . . ." He looked over at me. ". . . because of irrelevant matters."

"Don't be more of a fool than you have to be, Miguel. Unless you do it, David will, once he reaches his majority." She smiled warmly at me. "Won't you, David? Can't say as I blame you." She sniffed. "To think, putting out a reward for the death of an Elwerean."

"Leave it be, leave it be. The less it's talked about, the sooner it's forgotten." He glanced at his fingernail. "I've eaten enough. Best to keep a bit hungry. Enrico Mengual and I have a minor affair this evening."

"Just first blood, no?" She sipped at her tea, eyeing him over the rim of the cup.

"Yes." He fingered the scar over his collarbone. "Although I'm tempted to give him a scar that will run from his navel to his kidney."

"Who gave offense? As though I have to ask."

"I did."

"I knew it, you—"

"*By concatenation*, Therese, by concatenation." He raised an eyebrow.

Knowing that he was taking over my duel didn't slow Aunt Therese down. "You did, eh? Over what?"

"The usual," Father said, pointedly not looking at me.

The words hung in the air for a moment.

"Aunt Therese," I said, "it was my fault. Again."

She peered at me. "What happened this time?"

I shrugged. "I had a run-in with Erik Mengual, and he challenged me." Damn overbearing Elwerie—I hadn't meant to spill the glass of wine on his tunic, and he wouldn't accept my apology. Said he didn't think I meant it.

And, dammit, I had *so* been sincere. I knew that Father would end up fighting the duel for me, and I wasn't trying to get him cut up, despite our constant arguments over Amos van Ingstrand.

Father nodded. "When I replaced David, Enrico decided to exercise his right to replace Erik." He smiled thinly. "But wait until year after next. Erik reaches his majority, and he'll calm down." He snorted. "Or end up cooling down. To room temperature." He turned to me. "If you can do so subtly, please remind Erik that he reaches his majority before you do, and that he'll be subject to my sword then."

Aunt Therese stared first at me, and then at him. "Wonderful, Miguel. Just wonderful. You constantly harangue the boy for being socially inept—as he is," she said, softening her words with a smile, "and then you ask him to give a veiled warning. Are you looking to have another duel with Enrico? Wouldn't it be better to finish this one first? Or don't you have enough to do?"

Emilita reached over and patted my hand under the table. "Cousin," she said, smiling tolerantly, "you promised to show me this sword that you're so proud of, that you claim will win the competition at Latch Festival." She rose, adjusting her dress modestly, then gestured a goodbye first to her mother and then to my father as she slipped on her teak half-casque. Awkwardly, I mimicked her, and followed her out through the door.

Emilita was several years younger than I—I checked the birth records—but she seemed older. Almost everyone did.

"David," she said, as we walked down the carpeted public corridor toward the elevator, "you really shouldn't annoy him about it." She nodded a polite greeting as we passed a scowling fifty-year-old, one of her friends whom I didn't recognize.

"I want van Ingstrand dead." *And I want things to feel better than they do*, I thought. This was ridiculous. I'd spent my whole life dreaming about what it would be like to live in Elweré, and now I was here. . . .

And all it was was another place. A comfortable one, granted; a safe place, agreed. But just another one, not intrinsically better than where I'd lived before. Just cleaner, richer. The comfort, the not having to worry about where my next meal was coming from, that was nice. Very nice. It should have been enough. Why wasn't it?

"Wait a few years." She pressed her thumb to a touchplate; almost immediately the doors whisked open and we walked in. "You'll be able to handle it on your own. If you still care to. Which I beg to doubt." She moved aside to let me touch the plate. It immediately flashed green, which was just as well; the service staff had only about half the cars programmed to recognize my prints.

"My rooms, please," I said, staggering a bit as the elevator lurched sideways, then dropped. Despite years of Carlos' teaching and prodding, I still didn't have the map of Elweré solidly in my head; I never knew which way the damn elevators were going to go.

She scowled. "You don't have to be courteous to circuitry. It's there to serve."

"Like lowers."

"Of course." She nodded, genuinely surprised that I'd point out the obvious. "Except that circuits don't have a choice. The bourgeoisie and the lower classes do."

Some choice. The only wealth on Oroga came out of valda, and Elweré owned the valda. While some individuals among the lowers and buzhes could make their living elsewise, it all came down to having to serve Elweré, either directly or indirectly.

I've got to admit that didn't bother me. I was on the inside for once, and I liked it that way.

Still, there was an ache in me, a feeling of loss. Whether it was over Marie and Carlos, or whether I was missing the flashes of cherat with Eschteef, I don't know.

It could be that—

"David?" Emilita frowned up at me. "What is really bothering you? Other than van Ingstrand." She dismissed the notion of van Ingstrand's being worth worrying about with a toss of her head.

I shrugged. "I don't like Father fighting my duels for me."

Father was just too proud. He'd insist on substituting for me, but wouldn't insist on upgrading the duels to second blood. If he'd done that, I probably wouldn't have been challenged so often; the notion of facing Miguel Ruiz de Curdova in a first-blood affair didn't intimidate as many people as I wished it would have.

First-blood duels weren't all that dangerous; the worst result was likely to be only a few minutes of pain.

"It is his right, and his responsibility."

That didn't make me feel any better.

While my father's and my relationship was one mainly of duty, not affection, I still didn't want to see him getting hurt. Maybe even killed, unlikely as that was. In a first-blood duel as fought in Elweré, a good fencer was almost deathproof; safety-masked, with the physicians standing by, two centimeters of steel can kill you only if your opponent manages a clean thrust to the heart, the bladestop pushing in the flesh between the ribs. Father was too good and too smart to let that happen; he'd just take the point with his left hand, conceding the duel.

I sighed. I'd just have to wait awhile. Just awhile. Once the Metzadan fencing teacher arrived and helped me to become half-decent with a sword, maybe I'd be able to persuade Father to let me fight my own battles.

In not so many years I'd be able to do what I wanted, without permission. My sixtieth birthday wasn't *that* far off, although it would feel like a long fifteen years.

Fifteen years. It wasn't right that Amos van Ingstrand might live another fifteen years.

"David?"

"Eh?"

"We're here." She waved a hand at the elevator's open door. "You're drifting off again."

She followed me the few steps to my rooms. "Now, where's this sword you were telling me about?" she asked, as the door hissed shut behind us.

I tossed my casque in the corner. "You really want to see it?"

"No," she said, gracefully easing herself into a chair, doffing her own mask. "I'm sure it's very nice. I'm sure the schrift you bought it from did a fine job."

I shook my head. "I'm making it myself. With a little luck, I'll have it done by this Latch Festival that everyone's always talking about." I seated myself opposite her.

"Yourself?" She shrugged. "Why bother?"

"*Why bother?*" I started to rise from my chair, then let myself fall back. "Why bother? Because I'm so damn clumsy at everything else. Working with metal and jewels is one of the two things that I can do well."

"David—"

"The other thing I do well—and I do it *very* well—is stealing."

She reddened. I really shouldn't have said that. In Elweré, stealing isn't a crime, it's a perversion. "You're so unkind, David. I wasn't mocking you. It's just that if this sword is good, why show it at Latch Festival? Why not save it for another festival, or just give it to your father?"

"I . . . don't understand."

"It's *Latch* Festival that's coming up, David. You don't know about Latch Festival?"

The name was familiar, but I guess that I hadn't paid much attention to its mention in Esquela's book.

"It's a . . ." She paused, looking for the right words. Elweries always have trouble explaining Elwerie customs. I guess a fish might have a problem discussing water. "It's a demonstration of wealth, David. We bring things of value to the Grand Ballroom, and compare, contest over which is the finest."

I shrugged. "So? Maybe I'm not as good as a real schrift jeweler, but I don't think I'd embarrass myself."

"But David, after the competition, we destroy the entries. It . . . shows that we're wealthy, and that we can afford to."

I didn't hear her. Make something beautiful, even just buy something beautiful, only to destroy it?

That was perverted. That's not the way it's supposed to be. Beauty is supposed to last forever.

She reached over and touched my hand. "But this isn't why I wanted to talk to you."

"Well?"

"I'm going shopping in Lower City this afternoon. Is there anything you'd like me to bring back?" She spoke quietly, seriously.

"Van Ingstrand's head."

"No, seriously. Is—is there?"

She was serious about something, but I didn't have the slightest idea about what. Carlos' training in Elwerie customs had been oriented toward fitting in only superficially, just well enough and long enough to lift a few purses. Trying to *really* fit in wasn't the same thing. It was so damn frustrating.

"Emilita, what are you getting at?"

She looked away. "H-how long has it been since you've . . . been with a woman?"

"Emilita—" I caught myself in mid-chuckle. It was difficult enough for my cousin to bring up the subject.

At least this was something I understood; it was one of the few things that Esquela wrote about that wasn't totally opaque.

Death and Decadence Among the Elwereans, Chapter Five, "Sexual Mores," reads, in part: "There are few societies in which sexual promiscuity is as heavily practiced, and as little talked about, as the Elwerean society.

"The practices are almost schizoid in their nature; discussion of intercourse is taboo, as is the practice of intercourse among nondyadic individuals, with the sole exception of occasions during which the individuals are masked. The practice of masking creates the social fiction that it is the mask acting, and not the individual. However, even masked, discussions or practice of intercourse are forbidden in private (except, apparently, between regular dyadic partners), for there would be no third party present to swear that the individuals were masked. . . .

"Masked orgies are the norm for nondyadic intercourse, although Elweré men frequently resort to prostitutes among the non-Elweré population, again employing one of several creative fictions to obviate any admission that this indeed occurs. . . ."

All of which did damn little good to me right then and there. I'd been without Gina for a long time, and Emilita was, as I've said, both very attractive and revealingly dressed.

On occasion, she'd made it clear to me that she wouldn't at all mind if I made a point of picking her out of the crowd during a party.

But I didn't go to the parties, not after the first time. The one time I'd gone to one, I'd left nauseated. The sprawling couples on the floor, bodies covered with

wine and oil, intertwined . . . it all seemed so *ugly*.
Things were supposed to be different in Elweré.

As they were, I guess. But this wasn't what I'd thought
about when I thought that Elweré was different. "What
are you trying to say, Emilita?"

"I—I know that your father won't let you leave Elweré,
not yet. But if there's someone, someone in Lower City
you'd like to see? I . . . think I could arrange it, David.
Just for a few hours. Perhaps there is nothing that any
resident can do, but maybe some lower could help you
with your . . . problem. You wouldn't be afraid of . . .
being with a lower, would you?" She buried her face in
her hands.

My problem. I almost laughed. It all fit together. Poor
little Emilita, living such a sheltered life. She figured
that the reason I didn't go to the parties was that I was
somehow afraid of touching some Elwerie goddess.

*Emilita, with a lot of luck, perhaps someday that could be my
greatest problem.*

But maybe she had an idea. I couldn't go out and
talk things over with Eschteef, but maybe . . . "Her
name is Gina. I'll give you the address of the house
where she works. You sure you can bring her here?"

Still not looking directly at me, Emilita nodded. "Yes."

"When?"

"Maybe even later today. Perhaps tomorrow, or the
day after. But you should be sure to be ready before
Latch Festival. It's only a few days away, you know."

I started to ask why, but she blushed. Again.

I set the sword down on the durlyn work table and
looked at it. It was a meter-long saber, razor-sharp on
both true edge and false. The tracings of vines along
the flat of the blade still didn't stand out enough, so I
poured some more oxidant on a rag, wiped the blade
down to a dull black, and then turned on my buffer.

I buffed it off; the lines stayed dark, the rest of the blade mirror-bright.

Nice. It wouldn't make much of a fighting weapon. Eschteef had promised to teach me the trick of working other metals into the edge of a blade, making silver as hard as good steel, but it hadn't gotten around to it. The sword was for show, not for use.

It was a good piece of work. Still, a lot more work would have to go into it for it to be just right. It had a solid tang, but I hadn't quite decided what sort of hilt or basket I'd put on it.

I'd been trying out different sketches, hoping to get it ready.

Enough of that. More work might go into the sword, but no more work would go into getting it ready for the Latch Festival.

I snorted. The idea of creating something beautiful, something wondrous, only to have it destroyed as a demonstration of wealth . . .

"Idiots. I'm surrounded by idiots." Taking up a chamois, I did the final buffing by hand, enjoying the feel of the soft cloth slipping over the smooth surface.

Dimly, I could feel Eschteef's joy at the work of my hands—

No. That part of my life was over. I was home now. This was where I belonged. I was free here. Free of Carlos, free of Amos van Ingstrand, free of Eschteef's demands. Free. Not in a cage, not anymore.

I could almost hear Hrotisft's dry whisper. *And what is the difference, stupid human, between this cage and any other?*

"It's not a cage, dammit. I can go where I want."

Anywhere in Elweré. You have a large cage, and a comfortable one. But a cage, nonetheless.

"Leave me alone!"

But there was nobody there.

Time for a walk. I donned an informal casque, then ook a smallsword down from the wall and belted it on.

Alone, I walked through the crowded Promenade. At tables lining the eastern wall, overdressed and underdressed Elweries sat, sipping coffee, tea, and wine, chattering about jewels and clothes, festivals and entertainments.

My right arm felt naked without my blade and sheath. With all this wealth around, my natural tendency was to slice and run. The sword wasn't a substitute, although perhaps someday it would be. Fencing didn't come naturally to me. Maybe when the Metzadan instructor Father had hired actually arrived, he could teach me, but I doubted it.

What was the point? Why bother learning to use such an archaic weapon well? Just so nobody would elbow me pseudo-accidentally? Ridiculous. A blade should be only a few centimeters long, hidden in the hand, ready to snap into the palm for slicing the string of a purse or the tendons of an arm.

But why bother stealing, even for practice? My own pouch was filled with diamonds, emeralds, firestones, and rubies, all had for the asking.

For a moment, I considered taking the pouch and scattering the baubles across the floor. Instead, I walked across the marble floors, returning an occasional nod, not bothering to gesture a request for an invitation to join anyone.

Again, why bother? Discussions of clothes, and plays, and masques, drink, and duels didn't interest me. It never would. Ever.

At the high-arched entrance to the Grand Theater, the main screen showed offworld players frolicking on its stage. The tiny screen above it informed me that it was the Royal Shakespeare Company, doing *As You Like It*, and that the next performance would be at ten o'clock.

Shakespeare? That didn't sound familiar. It couldn't have been one of the Thousand Worlds; the only planetwide monarchy was on Rand. I couldn't recall a world named Shakespeare. Must have been some country or other. Might be worth looking up on the screen.

But that would be about all. Stretching out on a couch along with a thousand or so others, all to watch some idiot offworlders mumble some lines, was about as interesting as watching my fingernails grow.

So I kept walking, until I reached the Arena, taking a seat almost all the way up against the rear wall, well away from the few score watchers ringside. Clearly only a minor affair; death duels tend to draw a crowd.

Here was something I could understand. Not appreciate—fighting over imagined or real social slights is stupid—just understand.

Under the watchful eyes of a team of six harnessed buzh physicians, two Elweries squared off on the tarmac below. Both men were stripped to the waist, wearing little besides their wraparound facemasks, groincups, and sandals. Clearly a first-blood affair; even from this height I could see the tiny crossbars on the swords, just two centimeters from the needle-sharp points.

At the referee's signal, the two men crossed swords, dropped back, and saluted, dropping back into twin fighting stances.

Then they closed. There was a quick flash of steel, and one of the men staggered back, clapping his free hand to his shoulder, the sword dropping from his other hand.

And that was it. The other Elwerie turned and walked away while the six physicians rushed up to treat the loser.

Pointless, that's what it was. Just another silly game. I turned and walked away.

There were three main ballrooms off the Promenade. The largest one—the Grand Ballroom—abutted the Grand Theater. On the rare occasions that the performance in the theater drew a crowd large enough to lead to a shortage of couches, the wall separating the two was lowered into the floor, and more couches were brought in.

Usually, though, it was empty. The Grand Ballroom was just too large for most events.

I glanced at the screens outside the Grand Ballroom. The main one was blank, indicating that nothing was happening there at the moment; the smaller one informed me that a dance was scheduled for the evening. Another idiotic practice—the Elweries seemed to spend half their lives walking out figures on the floor in time to music. And not even decent, recorded music; usually live orchestras, complete with twittering, screeching strings and occasional fluffed notes from the brass instruments.

Well, I knew where I wasn't going to be that night. My dance teacher would have written me off as hopeless if he could have done so without losing his job. I wasn't exactly uncoordinated, but I couldn't see putting in any serious effort for that sort of nonsense.

The screens in front of the Bronze Ballroom had broken down; three harnessed buzh technicians were busy replacing them. I thought about asking what was going on inside, if anything, but decided not to. No point; I didn't have anything better to do than walk in and see for myself.

I walked through the entrance. Once past the sound-shields, the music and moans from inside hit me like a hammer.

Wonderful. I glanced inside, just to be sure.

There are times when I think that the schrift have point about human reproductive customs; in the Bronze Ballroom, several hundred Elweries were involved in a game of let's-find-the-orifice.

I turned away from the mass of writhing, oiled bodies—and was bumped to the ground.

A slim fifty-year-old stood above me, his half-casque revealing only the scowling lower portion of his face, his hands set on his hips. "Well," he said. "Have you nothing to say?"

Not again. I got to my feet. "My apologies. I did not intend to bump into you."

He shook his head. "Not good enough, not by half. You don't see fit to introduce yourself?"

"I am sorry. My name is David Curdova, and—"

"I see. You are the one raised by the lowers. Which explains your clumsiness, and your lack of manners; it does not excuse them. I am Luis Diego Muntoya." He raised his hand and tapped me lightly on the casque. "And you are challenged. I believe that your father will handle this affair on your behalf?"

I raised a hand. "Now, wait. He's already—"

"*Your father will choose to handle this affair on your behalf?*"

"Yes."

"Very well. I will speak to him. In the meantime, get out of my way." He didn't wait for me to do that; he just pushed me aside and walked into the ballroom.

I stepped back out into the Promenade.

Again. I'd done it *again*. Probably there was something I should have said, something I should have done, but—

My phone buzzed; I raised my wrist to my face. "Yes?"

"Senhor Curdova, the package is now ready for delivery."

"Package? I didn't order a package."

"It is a present from your cousin, Emilita."

Gina!

"Senhor Curdova?"

"Y-yes. Where, how—"

"If you will return to your suite, we may complete delivery."

Ignoring curious glances, I ran.

The two buzhes waited patiently by the door, the large wooden box on the aircushion dolly between them. They were dressed in normal tunics, wearing what looked like an Elwerie's defensive harness, but wasn't. It was just the opposite, really; instead of looking for external threats, activating shoulder-mounted powerguns if necessary, these harnesses monitored the wearers, deciding, several thousand times per second, whether or not the buzh wearing it was attacking an Elwerie. The circuits could deliver a graduated-voltage electric reminder for minor offenses, or set off a shaped charge against the buzh's breastbone for major ones.

They both ducked their heads at my approach.

"Senhor David Curdova?"

"This box is for me?" I thumbed the door open, ushering them in.

"Yes, senhor. We will wait outside the door, for when you are finished with the . . . merchandise."

"I don't think that will be necessary."

"It is required, senhor. Such merchandise must be returned to the outside before nightfall."

I nodded and let the door whisk shut in front of their faces, then spent a few seconds tearing my nails at the box's catch.

The front of the box fell open. Gina sat on the small bench inside, her arms crossed tight over her chest.

"It's about time," she said, smiling faintly.

"Gina—"

"We'd better talk about the money, first."

I opened my pouch and scattered the jewels on the carpet. "Enough?"

"Just barely," she said, as I offered her a hand out. "Just barely."

"You're quite the talk of Lower City, little David," she said quietly, her face buried against my chest. "Even old Amos was running scared for a while."

Amos van Ingstrand scared? Of me? "He damn well had better be."

She snorted. "*Was.* Until your father sent him the payment for killing Carlos." She sat up, drawing the sheets around her like a robe. "I think he's gone more than a little mad on the subject of you. When they do let you out, be careful. If there's a way around an Elwerean's defenses, he just might find it."

"If I ever go out. I'm not allowed. This place is a prison."

She glanced around the bedroom, taking in the tapestries and fixtures with a practiced eye. "Nice prison."

"Gina, I don't fit in here."

"Learn to."

I let the subject drop. "Tell me, how are things in Lower City? I'm really out of touch."

She smiled knowingly. "Oh, the usual. The new crop of mannafruit are a bit dry, there's been an increase in the payoff to the Protective Society, Alfreda's house is now catering to the leather trade—"

"Stop it. Gina, I need to talk to you."

"So talk." She shrugged. "It sounds like you want some pity." She held a thumb-sized diamond up to her

:ye. "You'd better look elsewhere for that. You didn't
pay me enough to pity you, Senhor Curdova. Looks to
ne like you've got a good deal here. Enjoy it."

And there it was. I couldn't enjoy it here. The words
umbled out. "This place isn't *right* for me. I don't fit
n. I don't know what these people want from me. I
don't want to stay here. I don't belong. My father is
going to get killed because I'm clumsy. They destroy
beautiful things just to show they can afford to. This—"

"Do me a favor and don't complain." She raised an
eyebrow. "If it bothers you that much, leave. I don't
care."

"I can't. The outside door wouldn't open for me, not
unless my father clears me."

"Just as well. If you go back into Lower City, Amos
would have you for breakfast." She smacked her lips.
"Maybe even literally."

"So I have to stay."

"Right." She snorted. "Be a victim. Idiot."

"What are you trying to say?"

"David, I like you. You're not all that bad-looking,
you're fun in bed . . ."

"I think I hear a but."

". . . *but,* you're a born victim. You stayed with Carlos
for most of your life, let him push you around."

"But I only did that for Marie."

"Nonsense. You've never done anything for anyone
else. You did that so that you wouldn't have to run
your life for yourself. Then you let Eschteef and the
rest of the schrift badger you—"

"How did you know about that?"

"Eschteef looked me up." She laughed. "And you
should have seen the looks I got. Matter of fact, my
prices went way up just after; all the offworlders figured that if I'm good enough to turn on a schrift—"

I grabbed her arms. "Why?"

"Why what? Why did Eschteef look me up? Th[e] stupid creature is worried about you. Figured that some[-] body from your own species might be able to give som[e] perspective." She shrugged. "And since I'm your onl[y] human friend . . ."

I sat up and let my legs dangle over the edge of th[e] bed.

This was ridiculous. I'd lived my whole life in depri[-] vation and fear. Here in Elweré, that could be over. [I] could forget everything.

So why did I keep hearing Eschteef saying, *You are o[f] my schtann, David?*

And Marie. . . .

"I've got to get out of here." I shook my head. "Bu[t] there isn't any way. Not now. Maybe, in a few years[,] after I seem to settle in, my father will let me, but—"

She snorted. "Whatever you do, *don't* take charge of your own life, David."

"What's that supposed to mean?"

She gestured toward the open door. "There's room enough in that box for the two of us. It'd be a bit cramped, but if you're really serious . . ."

I didn't stop to think about it; I just nodded. "We'll do it. Just one thing, first." I got out of bed and walked over to the delivery box.

"Going to find somebody to talk you out of it? Maybe get your father to prevent you from leaving?"

"No." I leaned over the delivery box. "One powergun, fully loaded, please. And three spare clips."

"Yes, senhor."

Her eyes widened. "Amos?"

"Amos."

She smiled. "Order up some more jewels, as long as you're at it. Hmmm, and some muslin, and thread. We'd better make you a tunic that isn't so flashy."

"Right." I ran to my workroom and wrapped my sword. It was too fine to leave in Elweré.

The box may have been roomy for one; even with the bench removed, it was awfully small for two. Gina's hipbone kept digging into one of my thighs, the power-gun into the other.

And the buzh handler wasn't any too gentle.

Finally, the hissing of the carrier stopped. "All right in there, we're out. Now, what'll you do for me if I open up the box?"

"Let me out!" Gina shrilled.

"C'mon, now, how about a little something for the working man—" the voice cut off into a strangled moan; the outside catches snicked loose.

‹Well, David? Do you like the cramped box? Or would you rather see the daylight?› The door swung open, and a familiar face peeked in.

"Eschteef!"

"Good guess." Gina snickered, blinking against the bright sunlight. She levered herself off my lap and out of the box.

I followed.

Eschteef stood on the bare dirt, one hand wrapped around the handler's throat. The human face was bright red; his eyes bulged as he clawed uselessly at the schrift's arm.

"How did you know?"

"You are of my schtann, David. The link is there, whether you admit it or not. I told this *Gina* that you would come." Eschteef was polite; he was talking in Basic for Gina's benefit.

"He even offered to bet." She smiled at me. "But I didn't like the odds."

I eyed the setting sun, then hitched at the powergun. "I'd better get going—"

‹No, little one. Not today.› He released the guard, who fell to the ground, choking. ‹It is too close to sundown. We will deal with Amos van Ingstrand tomorrow.›

"We?"

‹Yes, David, we. You are of my schtann, and Amos van Ingstrand has threatened you. But for now, we had best decide where you will spend the night.›

"I figured I'd stay at home." Home. That was a strange word, but Eschteef's cul-de-sac was my home, dammit. Not Elweré.

"No. I am involved in some work that will keep me busy well through midday tomorrow; you would not be able to sleep."

"I don't mind not sleeping—"

Gina elbowed me in the side. "Since you're not going to sleep anyway, maybe you'd like to not do it somewhere else? If you've got some coin, that is. I don't come cheap by the night, you know."

"Fine." I smiled, tossing her a diamond from my pouch. "This enough?"

"For now."

Eschteef hissed. "You must explain all this to me sometime."

She cocked her head to one side. "If you have to ask, you won't understand it. Let's get out of here."

SIXTH INTERLUDE:

Eschteef

The child would not be left alone, Eschteef thought, sitting in front of its workbench. There would be two groups after it: the Elwereans, who would want David back in the city; and Amos van Ingstrand's Protective Society, still holding a grudge for the youngling's having stolen van Ingstrand's brooch.

The Elwereans could be handled. There was no cherat between them and David; a simple change in the child's appearance could fool them. Possibly, Eschteef could plant a rumor that David had left Oroga. Hmm ... that could be done easily.

In any case, even if they failed to fool the Elwereans, the worst possible result would be David's temporary return to the city. No danger; just some inconvenience in getting it out again, perhaps a delay of a few years.

Hmmm ... actually, leaving Oroga had its virtues.

But that would require getting the child past the Protective Society guards near the 'port. It would also require persuading David that leaving Oroga was the best thing to do.

And it would also be necessary to *decide* whether or not leaving Oroga was the best thing to do. Here, David was at least around members of his schtann and members of his species; on Schriftalt, the child would have only members of his schtann to deal with, and they would not recognize him as such. The child still felt no cherat with the rest of the schtann.

Eschteef leaned back and tasted the deep cherat, reveling in its warmth. Something would have to be done about the child; it was not right that David couldn't feel this.

There was no way of telling how long it would take for cherat to develop between David and the rest; there had never been a human member of the schtann before. Perhaps it would have to grow into the bond, into the mindlink.

That might take some time. In the meantime, there was still Amos van Ingstrand to worry about.

Possibly van Ingstrand would leave David alone out of fear of retribution from David's provider-of-the-moving-part-of-the-egg. But that might not result in van Ingstrand's leaving the child alone; it might merely make it careful.

Not good; not acceptable.

But the child was of the schtann, and van Ingstrand would fear the schtann . . . but only if the human truly believed that.

And how could it believe that David is of my schtann? How can I make Amos van Ingstrand believe it, when even Hrotisft does not?

But there had to be a solution. The child had cost Amos van Ingstrand both prestige and money. The money could be replaced, but not the prestige.

Eschteef's eye fell on its chrostith. Unless . . .

CHAPTER ELEVEN:

"We Heard You...."

I woke slowly in the morning light, Gina still asleep beside me. Dawn sunlight streamed through the windows and splashed on the bed.

I was only half awake, but my mind was already starting to work.

I wasn't going to go back to Elweré. That was just another prison. Safer than living with Carlos, more comfortable than living with Carlos, but just another cage.

I couldn't stay here, not after Eschteef and I killed van Ingstrand; his people wouldn't take kindly to that, and I could hardly call upon my father for his protection. For that matter, I could hardly call upon my father at all. He wouldn't understand. Elweré felt right—maybe it was right—for him, for Emilita.

But not for me. I let my head loll back on the pillow. Not for me.

Might as well sleep in for a while, I thought. I wouldn't be able to talk to Eschteef until he finished whatever project he was on. Besides, before leaving I'd have to send Gina out to buy some supplies; going out without makeup was just asking for trouble.

I slept.

*　　*　　*

I dreamed, and as I dreamed, the room I was in shrank, the fat human in front of me becoming smaller than I was, instead of larger.

Why were my arms bound behind me? For some reason or other, I was bargaining with van Ingstrand for my freedom, trying to buy his vengeance with something that no human had ever possessed.

That seemed silly; buying off vengeance wasn't a human sort of thing to do.

He knew that. He smiled, raised a knife, and stabbed it into my leathery chest, again, and again.

I came awake with a start. *Eschteef!* "No." It wasn't a dream. Van had Eschteef; he was hurting it.

But how? Why?

It didn't matter. I threw on my tunic, belting it tightly, then slipped the powergun into it, snatching up the spare clips and tucking them into my pouch as I sprinted from the room.

Vague visions of a knife rising and falling superimposed themselves over my eyes as I ran through the hall and down the staircase; I staggered, and almost tumbled headlong down the steps.

By the time I reached the street, the mindlink was gone.

Eschteef was dead. I was all alone again.

No—wait. Maybe it was just unconscious. I didn't have enough experience with cherat; maybe it couldn't break through to an unconscious mind.

I felt cold and miserable. Normal.

Gina called out after me as I ran down the street, the dirt hard and cold under my bare feet, the occasional pebble sending me into a half-run, half-hop.

I ignored all that. I had to think it through. If Eschteef wasn't dead, I'd have to get to it quickly. If I could do it. If I could get inside the house, if I could get past van

Ingstrand's guards, if one of the schtann could save its life—if, if, if. Lives shouldn't always have to depend on those goddam ifs.

Wait! I couldn't feel myself part of the schtann, but Eschteef wasn't a cripple. Even if the mindlink wouldn't work while it was unconscious, the schtann would have heard Eschteef before, when I had; others would already be on the way to help it.

I allowed myself to slow down, glaring at the passersby as they gave me curious glances. I had to work this out. Maybe I should just leave things be, for now. When the schtann rushed van Ingstrand's house, it might be best for me not to be there at all. The schrift wouldn't necessarily recognize me as friendly; they might not recognize me at all.

I stopped at the fountain and splashed some water on my face. Across the square, Arno the mannafruit vendor shouted and waved at me, careful not to call me by name.

Maybe I should go over to Arno, talk to him. Just let the schtann handle van Ingstrand. Let them get revenge for me, for Marie, and Eschteef, and even for Carlos.

Right. That's all I had to do. Just let them handle it. After all, what did I owe Eschteef? It had chained me, and threatened my life.

And forced me to learn how to create beauty and wonder, and had tried to break me out of the prison of my mind. Eschteef had believed in me and trusted me, and was likely dead because of me.

No. I wouldn't leave van Ingstrand for the schtann.

I ran.

Van Ingstrand's house was just beyond the end of Baker's Row, one of a dozen similar buzh homes, this one separated by ten extra meters from its neighbors, as though the other houses were shying away in fear.

I ducked behind a neighboring porch and tried to catch my breath, tried to stop my heart from beating a triphammer staccato in my chest.

How could I get into the house? There was no obvious way; the windows were barred, shuttered and likely bolted from inside. The large front door was closed, and certainly guarded.

And where the hell was the schtann? There was nobody out on the street here. There should have been at least dozens of schrift breaking down van Ingstrand's doors.

Maybe they hadn't heard Eschteef? Maybe Eschteef's mindlink with me interfered with cherat with the rest of the schtann? Was that possible?

I didn't know. I just didn't have enough information. But I couldn't rely on the schtann to get Eschteef out of there, if he was still alive, or even to avenge him, if he was dead.

I'd handle it. And not just for Eschteef. For Marie, and myself—and even Carlos.

I ran around behind van Ingstrand's house. The brickwork here was pitted. Plenty of finger and toe holds. Wishing for my climbing gloves, I worked my way to the roof and pulled myself over the edge, gasping for breath as I lay there.

No time to rest. I forced myself to my feet. The top of the roof was empty, save for a trapdoor. A swift tug persuaded me that it was securely bolted.

I shrugged, drawing the powergun. Bolts and hinges could be broken.

But I'd have to move fast, get inside as quickly as possible, as soon as I blew off the door.

I thumbed the power on and the safety off, taking a spare clip from my pouch and holding it in my mouth. When the tiny electrical charge tickled the first of the weapon's sileohalcoid rounds, the hair-thin wire would stretch almost instantly, springing back to its normal shape, zipping out of the barrel as part of the recoil brought the next round into firing position. It would have quite a kick; I'd have to be careful to keep the weapon trained on the target.

I barely touched the trigger; the gun jerked in my hands, drawing a skittering line across the roof, not damaging the bolt at all.

Not good. I held the gun more firmly, pointing it directly at one of the trapdoor's hinges, and tried again.

This time it worked; the stream of wires tore the hinge to shreds. I adjusted my aim and fired again, shattering the other hinge with one continuous blast.

The clip was running low; I slipped it out of the handle, slammed a fresh clip home, and thumbed the safety off again before moving next to the trapdoor. I had to do this just right.

I kicked the trapdoor; it sagged. Another kick, and it fell into the building. I jumped in after it.

Directly into a net. A fist came out of nowhere, knocking the powergun out of my hands. The last thing I remember was feet kicking me, over and over.

The one time in my life I woke quickly, it was to see Amos van Ingstrand leering down at me, a broad smile creasing his fat face.

"It is good to see you, David." A flipperlike hand patted my cheek. "I have waited a long time for this moment." His smile broadened.

I was flat on my back, staring up at him, my hands tied over my head, my waist, knees, and ankles strapped. I could see myself in the full-length mirror above and behind van Ingstrand's head.

I didn't look any too good. The right side of my face was swollen and purple; blood from minor wounds dotted my tunic. I moaned as my cheek pulsed with pain; I tasted salt, and felt the fragments of shattered teeth in my lower jaw.

Van Ingstrand turned to look at someone outside my field of view. "Quiet, isn't he?" He smiled down at me. His face, broad and almost cherubic, gleamed with sweat in the candlelight. "Don't you have anything to say? Anything at all?"

I spat broken bits of teeth up at him, choking on a piece that didn't go in the right direction. No point in saying anything; it would just make him enjoy it more.

"Nothing to say, eh?" he tsked. "And I was so looking forward to you saying something about how your father won't tolerate my hurting you, how I can't get away with this."

Hope brightened. That was right! My father wouldn't let him get away with this; if I just disappeared in Lower City he'd attribute it to van Ingstrand. And van Ingstrand knew that; he wouldn't dare—

Van Ingstrand smiled. "But I can, and I will." He produced a flat plastic rectangle. "A ticket off Oroga, David. Your ticket. Officially, you're going to be leaving in just a few hours. Actually, I expect you'll be around for many days. Many days."

His broad face was beatifically innocent. "Your son, senhor? Of course I wouldn't dare touch the young lad, senhor. Would you like help in finding him? Every resource of the Protective Society is at your disposal—" The mask dropped. "Bring the candle closer," he said. "Don't worry if a few drops fall on little David here. That might be a nice touch. He will be with us for a long time."

"We will have plenty of time with this one, Mr. van Ingstrand," the other said. "It won't be like it was with Owen. I promise."

Van Ingstrand nodded. "I have an Elwerean medikit here, David. You will certainly last days. Perhaps"—he clapped his hands together with a meaty thunk—"weeks. Perhaps no one except Mikos here will know what I did to the boy who stole from me, but that isn't important. Everyone else already knows how I dealt with Carlos and the little girl; what happens to you will be our little secret."

He picked up a scalpel and stuck it into my arm. He did it casually, just the way I'd pick up and use a fork. I opened my mouth to scream; van Ingstrand wadded a cloth inside, almost choking me.

"You won't tell, will you?" His friendly facade dropped as he turned to his assistant. "What is it, Mikos?"

"Umm, Mr. van Ingstrand, I'm a bit nervous about having this other body around. Would you like me to get rid of—"

"Be silent, Mikos. I've always thought this schrift telepathy was overrated. Just tell the guards to keep their eyes open and their weapons ready. If any of the lizards try to break in, they can join David on the table."

"Yes, sir."

Amos van Ingstrand waddled out to my line of sight. "I have something to show you, before we begin." A power blade whined.

"Do you want me to tilt him up?" Mikos asked.

"A good idea." Van Ingstrand's voice practically glowed. "Let him see all of it."

I heard catches unlatching behind me, and the table swung up. If I hadn't been strapped to it, I would have fallen; as it was, I sagged against the straps.

In front of me, Amos van Ingstrand, panting from the exertion, merrily sawed at Eschteef's neck. Blood flowed slowly from the cuts.

"Oh, he's crying, Mikos. Wipe his eyes. I want him to see this. All of it."

I closed my eyes tightly. *Make it go away.*

A knifepoint pricked my neck. "Open your eyes. Mr. van Ingstrand wants you to watch."

My lids snapped open.

The room was dark, windowless; most likely we were in the basement under van Ingstrand's house. The door was made of steel, and bolted. The only light was from a candelabra overhead and another on the table to my right.

No escape. Even if I wasn't tied down, I wouldn't have been able to make it to the door before Mikos or van Ingstrand grabbed me. Ribs grated as I breathed; I wasn't in any condition to fight or run.

Van Ingstrand looked over at me and chuckled. "I could have electric lights down here . . ." The saw whirred. ". . . but the effect of the candles is pleasant, no?"

He picked up the head and held it in front of me. Eschteef's eyes, once bright and alive, stared glassily up at me.

"Look at the reward for stupidity, David. Your schrift friend came to me; he wanted to buy off my revenge against you, said he would give me gold, and silver, and jewels. Promised that he'd see to it that you didn't bother me for having your friends killed. All I had to do was to give up on hurting you. He thought it was just a matter of business with me."

Van Ingstrand set the head on the ground. "It isn't just business; it isn't even my hobby. Not with you, David. This will be something . . . special."

Even if I'd had my blade, and even if I could have snapped it into my hand, and even if I could have started to saw myself loose, it wouldn't have saved me.

I was going to die here, strapped to this table, and I was going to die alone. Alone. The way I'd lived.

There was only one chance, only one possible way out. If I could finally feel myself a part of the schtann, I could use the cherat, broadcast my distress to the others. If they felt the cherat with me, they might come to my rescue.

I had to do it. There was no other way.

But I couldn't. It meant dying, dying horribly; it meant that the only people I loved wouldn't ever be avenged, and I still couldn't feel part of something, I couldn't.

How do you *make* yourself feel something? It can't be done, not even when it's something you ought to feel. Not even when your life depends on it.

"But of course, there is a business side to it. I'm now respected, David," he said, walking out of my line of sight, "more than I ever have been. People have heard about Carlos, and your little Marie." He snickered. "Do you know what your slimy friend tried to buy me off with?"

There was a tapping as though of a fingernail on a metal bowl or—*no!*

Van Ingstrand walked back around the table, Eschteef's chrostith dangling casually from one hand, a ball-peen hammer in his other. "This. A water pitcher. That's what the filthy lizard offered me, as though it was something special. Said that nobody had ever been offered one of these before—and all it is is a pitcher!"

He let it slip out of his fingers and fall to the floor. It bounced three times, each bounce a slash to my heart.

"A stupid pitcher!" Van Ingstrand raised his hammer.

No, not that. Please. We all die. Every one of us has to; there's no way around it. There wasn't a way around it for Marie, Carlos, and Eschteef, and there won't be for me. But the beauty, the wonder we create . . . that's supposed to live on. Please. It just has to.

"Please. Don't."

He nodded. "A reaction, at last, eh?" Gently, he tapped the hammer against Eschteef's chrostith.

I couldn't even close my eyes. "No. Don't."

Van Ingstrand raised the hammer again, and brought it down on the pitcher.

It caved in like a piece of foil.

Anguish and anger rose, almost drowning me. The pain in my side and jaw was nothing compared to this. I struggled, trying to free myself from my bonds. This had to be stopped. It couldn't be allowed. *Kill me, but please, no, not this. I won't let—*

Something broke deep inside me. The walls in my mind shattered, disappeared as though they had never been.

I wasn't alone anymore; the schtann—no, *my* schtann— was with me. As it always could have been, if only I'd reached out for it. And as it always would be, for the rest of my life, and beyond.

‹We come, David,› Hrotisft said. ‹We will be there in moments.›

Sthtasfth voiced a mental protest. ‹No. Van Ingstrand will hear our approach; it must be distracted.›

‹Feel with it!› Threstast interrupted. ‹The child weakens; it must be strengthened.›

‹Yes.›

My mind sang a hymn of warmth and caring. Waves of reassurance washed over me in a loud benediction.

There was a clattering on the floor above us. Van Ingstrand turned toward the door.

‹Look at me, Amos van Ingstrand,› my mouth said. I wondered at the power of my own voice. And the words. Where were they coming from? I wasn't trying to say anything.

"What?" He turned back to me, stunned. "What do you think—"

Through my broken teeth, I smiled. ‹You will not harm another of my schtann. You will never harm another of my schtann.›

His face whitened. "But you—"

‹The dead harm no one.›

The steel door burst inward, the bar and hinges shattering. Like a gray flood, the schrift flowed in, carrying van Ingstrand and his man out of my sight. They only had time to scream once.

Flesh rended beneath strong hands and sharp teeth.

The rest of the schtann dined, while Hrotisft walked from behind and stood in front of me, its mouth bloody. ‹It is as I should have known,› it said. ‹Eschteef was correct about you, keh?›

Its old fingers were steady and sure as it removed my bonds, and helped me down from the board.

I tried to block out the pain. There was so much to be said, so much that I had to know.

But I was too badly injured. My right ankle must have been broken when van Ingstrand's guards kicked me unconscious; it gave way. I staggered, and almost fell.

Instantly, Sthtasfth was at my other side, adding a massive arm to support me. Blood dripped from its chin as it towered over me. With its other hand, it scooped the black medikit from the floor, not bothering to loosen the catch as it ripped the bag open. ‹Do you know how to use this *medikit*, David?› it asked, its loud voice somehow immeasurably gentle. ‹I do not have the knowledge.›

‹Valda oil,› Hrotisft said. ‹There should be a vial of valda oil. That will deal with the pain.›

‹But it tires. And there are many injuries,› Rhathsfoosf said, putting a dry hand against my forehead. ‹And it has suffered much pain. We must take it to one of its own species.›

‹The carrier of the breeding pond,› Threstast suggested, ‹the *female* that Eschteef mentioned—it might be able to help.›

"Yes," I said, my head spinning. "Gina. Take me to Gina."

It was just too much. I gave up and let the world go away.

CHAPTER TWELVE:

"This Is Just a Piece of Silver. . . ."

I sat on the bed next to the window, cradling the crumpled piece of silver in my arms. The pain was gone now, at least the pain in my body. Gina had done a decent job of doctoring while I was unconscious, but there hadn't been all that much to do. My ankle was just sprained, and the cuts needed only a few stitches. She'd had to pull the remains of a few broken teeth, but cauterization had sealed up those wounds, and valda oil prevented the pain.

Granted, I would need a bit of reconstruction, but that wasn't what bothered me.

Ignoring the three in the room with me, I looked through the barred window, out into the night.

Against a sea of stars, three t'Tant fluttered, hunting. Below them, all of Lower City spread out in the darkness.

And beyond that, the bright lights of Elweré.

I wept. That was all that there was to do.

‹David,› Hrotisft said. ‹We must talk.›

"What's there to talk about?" I lowered the battered remains of Eschteef's chrostith to the bed.

"Listen to them," Gina said, taking my hand. "Listen to them."

‹You must listen to us,› Sthtasfth said. ‹We are one, David.› It reached into its pouch, and produced a finely wrought jade pendant, and stared at the microscopic tracings across its surface. ‹This is my chrostith. My second. Which is finer than that which was my first chrostith, but not as fine as my third one will be. I bid you appreciate it with me.›

I felt Sthtasfth's joy. It had worked long and hard on the pendant, taking scraps of silver and unworked jade, and then turning it into wonder.

And, in another part of my mind, I could feel the rest of the schtann—not just here, but on worlds scattered across the sky—joining in my appreciation, basking in Sthtasfth's joy at the work of its hands. I was with all the others: the living, the dead, and the yet-to-live. I wasn't alone anymore.

Yes, now I was part of the schtann, but that wasn't enough. I'd ruined everything. For myself, for Marie, for Eschteef—

‹Mourn your little friend if you must, David. I understand that is good for humans to do, to let themselves feel hurt at the loss of those they cared for. But do not mourn Eschteef. It gambled that either it would be able to buy van Ingstrand's revenge, or that its death would break the bonds closing your mind to us.› Hrotisft picked up the remains of Eschteef's chrostith and held the battered heap of silver for a moment, then handed it to me. ‹And while it was the destruction of this pitcher and not Eschteef's death that made that happen, remember that Eschteef won its gamble. Do not mourn it, David. It died having served its schtann well. What more could anyone ask?›

I fingered the remains of Eschteef's chrostith. It had been so beautiful.

"He can't stay here," Gina said. "I mean, tonight isn't a problem, but if his father finds him, he'll make David go back to Elweré. He'd go crazy in there. Besides, Amos van Ingstrand and the others you killed weren't the whole Protective Society; you'll have to keep an eye out for whoever replaces him."

Easily solved. Hrotisft dismissed the problem with a sniff. "The schtann will pay for David's passage off Oroga. It can leave in the morning."

Off Oroga? "Where?" Where do you go to run away from yourself?

Hrotisft gestured at the window. ‹Look.› Above, the stars twinkled in the sky. ‹There are more than a thousand worlds out there, David. The schtann is on many of them. You have much to learn, little human. And I have a few years left in which to teach you.›

‹But what do we do?›

‹For tonight, mourn your dead, if you need to. Tomorrow, we will leave for Schriftalt. You have a need to be with more of your schtann than is anywhere else. And after that, who knows? I've heard that there is much need for good work on Earth.›

‹I have heard that, too,› Sthtasfth said. ‹Besides, David is human. It would be good for it to see the world from which its species came.›

‹I will show it to David. And see it with its eyes.›

‹You are going with me?›

‹Of course.› Hrotisft hissed. ‹You are far too young, weak, and ignorant to be left alone.›

‹And I will go, too,› Sthtasfth said. ‹You are far too old to teach it precision work, Hrotisft. The young one will need to learn from others.›

Hrotisft hissed. ‹And you need to teach, Sthtasfth.›

‹Of course. Is all this acceptable to you, David?›

I didn't answer. I cradled the remains of the pitcher in my arms.

‹Give me the silver,› Hrotisft said. ‹It is useless as it is. It will be melted down, and once again molded into beauty.›

"But Eschteef's chrostith!" I protested, holding it

tighter. "You can't melt down Eschteef's chrostith, not his masterwork. You *can't*."

‹True. I cannot. And I would not.›

Sthtasfth rested its hand on my shoulder. ‹Of course not. Eschteef's chrostith will become better every year. It is finally what it ought to be, part of its schtann. And its schtann will care for it, and teach it, and require the best of it. I foresee interesting times for Eschteef's chrostith, David.›

"I . . . don't understand."

‹David,› Hrotisft said. ‹Now, this thing is just a piece of silver. You are Eschteef's chrostith.›

ABOUT THE AUTHOR

Joel Rosenberg was born in Winnipeg, Manitoba, Canada, in 1954, and raised in eastern North Dakota and northern Connecticut. He attended the University of Connecticut, where he met and married Felicia Herman.

Joel's occupations, before settling down to writing full-time, have run the usual gamut, including driving a truck, caring for the institutionalized retarded, bookkeeping, gambling, motel desk-clerking, and a two-week stint of passing himself off as a head chef.

Joel's first sale, an op-ed piece favoring nuclear power, was published in *The New York Times*. His stories have appeared in *Issac Asimov's Science Fiction Magazine*, *Perpetual Light, Amazing Science Fiction Stories*, and TSR's *The Dragon*.

Joel's hobbies include backgammon, poker, bridge, and several other sorts of gaming, as well as cooking; his broiled butterfly leg of lamb has to be tasted to be believed.

He now lives in New Haven, Connecticut, with his wife and the traditional two cats.

The Sleeping Dragon and *The Sword and the Chain*, the first two novels in Joel's *Guardians of the Flame* series, are also available in Signet editions.

SIGNET Science Fiction You'll Enjoy

Great Science Fiction by Robert Adams from SIGNET

Buy them at your local
bookstore or use coupon
on next page for ordering.

More SIGNET Books by Arthur C. Clarke